I0646692

KEITH FINNEY

A NORFOLK MYSTERY

MURDER RSVP

By Keith Finney

The Norfolk Mysteries

For Joan

Vinci Books

vinci-books.com

Published by Vinci Books Ltd in 2025

1

Copyright © 2024 by Keith Finney

The author has asserted their moral right to be identified as the author of
this work in accordance with the Copyright, Designs and Patents Act 1988.
This work is a work of fiction. Names, characters, places and incidents are
the product of the author's imagination or are used fictitiously. Any
resemblance to actual persons, living or dead, places and incidents is
entirely coincidental.
All rights reserved. No part of this publication may be copied, reproduced,
distributed, stored in any retrieval system, or transmitted in any form or by
any means, including photocopying, recording, or other electronic or
mechanical methods, nor used as a source for any form of machine
learning including AI datasets, without the prior written permission of the
publisher.
The publisher and the author have made every effort to obtain permissions
for any third party material used in this book and to comply with copyright
law. Any queries in this respect should be brought to the attention of the
publisher and any omissions will be corrected in future editions.
A CIP catalogue record for this book is available from the British Library.
Paperback ISBN: 9781036700997

Chapter One

AN INVITATION

Wednesday, 3rd September: 10.00 am

AMID THE SWEET scent of peonies, Lyn Blackthorn's laughter floated through the air. She delighted in tying another pastel ribbon around the oak banisters of Stanton Hall, the ancestral home of her husband to be, Anthony Stanton. Lyn effortlessly moved around ladders and tables filled with wedding items, her shoulder-length blond hair tied back in a messy bun.

'Ant, do you think we've got enough bunting?' Lyn called out, her voice bright with excitement. She stood on tiptoes to adjust a stubborn floral arrangement, her 5' 6' frame stretched to its limit.

'Enough to wrap around Stanton Hall twice over,' Ant replied with an affectionate chuckle, his hands occupied with a tangle of fairy lights. The anticipation for their big day shone in his eyes like the mid-morning sun glinting off the nearby broad.

Just then, the grand doors of the Great Hall creaked open, and in sauntered the Earl and Countess Stanton like a gentle summer breeze. The Earl, tall and erect at 6'1', despite the ravages of age and ailments, shared a warm, easy-going smile with the couple.

'Dad, you look the bee's knees!' Ant said, noticing the crisp lines of his father's morning suit, a blend of timeless tradition and modern style.

'Only trying to match the splendour of what's being created here,' the earl said. He gestured to the festoons of decorations and transforming the enormous room.

The countess approached Lyn gracefully and with a warm smile. 'My dear, everything looks positively enchanting,' she said, her sharp mind already noting every detail laid out before her.

'Aw, thank you. It wouldn't have been possible without your guidance,' Lyn replied. Her laid back nature blended seamlessly with her surroundings. She knew that the support from Ant's parents was unwavering, as it was loving.

'Now, dear Lyn. Don't you think it's time you called me mum?' Her tone carried the wisdom of her years mixed with genuine affection.

'Then it must be dad for me,' the earl chimed in. He placed a hand on Ant's shoulder, conveying a father's pride and a sense of deep love to the young couple.

'Mum, Dad,' Lyn corrected herself, her cheeks tinged with colour.

As they turned to admire a display of wedding favours, the wind outside picked up, playfully tossing leaves against the windows. It seemed to serve as a reminder of the ever-present dance between change and the steadfast nature of tradition. Inside Stanton Hall, the promise of new beginnings filled the air, mingling with the laughter and chatter of the wedding preparations.

'Can you believe it?' Ant mused, his arm slipping around Lyn's waist. 'On Saturday, all this will come alive with friends and family.'

'As you say,' the earl agreed, his gaze drifting nostalgically around the ancient hall. 'And our little slice of history welcoming your future together.'

'Here's to the bride and groom,' the countess raised an imaginary glass, her eyes twinkling, 'And to traditions that stand the test of time.'

They immersed themselves once more in the joyous task at hand, unaware of the danger that would soon cast itself over their idyllic preparations.

————

Wednesday, 3rd September: 2.00 pm

THE AMBER GLOW of the Wherry Arms pub enveloped Ant, Lyn, and their longtime friend, Fitch. As usual, they occupied their favourite corner of the village hostelry. Outside, the breeze toyed with the thatched roof, a playful whisper against the sturdy walls of the centuries-old establishment.

'Ah, nothing like a drink with mates after a day of wedding madness,' Lyn sighed contentedly, her blond hair catching the dim lighting in soft waves.

'I agree,' Ant replied, his eyes alight with mirth as he watched the popular pub fill with locals. 'Imagine, in four days' time, you'll officially become a Lady of the Manor.'

Fitch chuckled, raising his pint in a toast. 'To Viscount

Anthony and Viscountess Stanton. May your reign be long and filled with fewer surprises than your sleuthing days brought you.'

Lyn laughed, her temperament shining through even as she pondered their future. 'I'll settle for a quiet first week before we dive into our roles. The last thing we need is the village thinking we're bringing a whirlwind of change on our very first day. As for the sleuthing, those days are behind us now.'

'Change is good,' Ant countered gently, his gaze fond as he considered his bride-to-be. 'Besides, if anyone can win over the village, it's you. Headteacher and now Lady of the Hall; you've got quite the fan club.'

'Speaking of change,' Fitch interjected, 'have you given any more thought to those renovations at the hall you mentioned a couple of months ago?'

'Slowly but surely,' Ant nodded. 'We want to respect the past, yet there's no denying the allure of central heating on a frosty morning.'

'Or reliable Wi-Fi,' Lyn added with a smile. 'Imagine your dad trying to stream his favourite historical documentaries with the current setup. It'd be easier to summon the spirits of his ancestors for a live reenactment.'

They shared a chuckle, the trio all too aware of the earl's endearing struggles with technology.

'Still,' Ant mused, the humour fading from his voice as a shadow of concern crossed his features, 'We have to tread carefully. The Hall is grade two listed, so we can't so much as knock a nail in without council approval.'

'Ah, but that's where you excel, my friend,' Fitch said reassuringly. 'You'll navigate those choppy waters with the grace of an old sea captain.'

'I'm more focused on not tripping over my dress on

Saturday than the intricacies of listed building planning permissions,' Lyn added with a giggle.

'Here's to not tripping, then,' Fitch raised his glass again, an impish twinkle in his eye.'

'Cheers to that,' Ant echoed, clinking his glass against the others. 'Now, let's enjoy this calm before the storm of festivities on Saturday, shall we?'

'Agreed,' Lyn smiled.'

As the playful banter between lifelong friends continued, Jed, the landlord, picked his way through a crowded bar towards the merry trio. He carried twin envelopes of creamy vellum. The Wherry Arms, a haven of oak beams and laughter, had seen its share of mysteries, but none so curious as the missives now carried across its worn stone flagstones.

'Ant, Lyn,' Jed called out, 'Seems you've got mail.'

Lyn's eyes lifted from her half-finished pint of lemonade, curiosity piquing her lips into a tentative smile. Ant turned, a spark of intrigue lighting the depths of his ocean-blue eyes.

'Post?' Lyn quipped; head tilted. 'Who'd be sending us letters here, I wonder?'

'I didn't get a proper look at the lad,' Jed replied, setting the envelopes on the small, round table. His voice, usually a jovial bellow, dipped into a hushed tone, as though the paper demanded reverence. 'He left them on the bar then scarpered before I could say boo.'

Ant reached for the envelopes, fingers brushing against the thick paper. A seal pressed into the wax caught his eye— a symbol unrecognisable, neither family crest nor familiar motif. He exchanged a glance with Lyn, their shared excitement tinged with uncertainty.

'Odd, isn't it?' Lyn said, her easy-going nature wrestling

with the wariness that crept up her spine. 'To receive invitations, isn't it? And without a face to attach them to.'

'Invitations or otherwise,' Ant said, thumbing the edge of one envelope, 'it's the timing that has me puzzled. Four days before our wedding, and here we are, about to open two curious invitations.'

'Perhaps they're just late in replying,' Fitch chimed in, ever the beacon of optimism. 'A straggler hoping for a seat at the feast?'

'Or a late gift, wrapped in secrecy,' said Lyn confidently, yet her hand hesitated to break the seal.

'Either way, it seems we're to be the stars in our own little English mystery.' Ant's attempt at humour didn't quite mask the undercurrent of tension. The wind outside picked up, rattling the windows as if to underscore the drama within.

'Then let's not keep our audience waiting.' Lyn drew a deep breath, her decision made, her gaze meeting Ant's with resolute clarity. With careful fingers, she pried open the first envelope, the sound of tearing paper echoing like a muted prelude to the unknown.

'Steady on,' Ant murmured, a protective edge to his voice as he echoed Lyn's actions with the second envelope. His former service in the military had attuned him to danger.

They opened the envelope together, their faces showing a mix of curiosity and nervousness.

'Let's see what secrets these whispers carry,' Lyn said bravely. Her pulse quickened, the anticipation building a suspenseful pause in the cozy haven of the pub.

Lyn's fingers paused as she unfolded the parchment. The ancient wisp of paper that seemed at odds with the jovial clinking of pint glasses and the low murmur of conversation around them. Ant watched, his own invitation lying flat against the dark wood of the table, a silent spectre amidst the warm glow of the pub.

'Heavens,' Lyn exclaimed, her voice a ghostly thread in the suddenly still air. The invitation carried no festive news, no joyful summons to friends and family. Instead, a ghastly depiction of Stanton Hall, etched in ink so black it leeched warmth from the room.

'Read it aloud,' Ant urged, though the unease in his voice betrayed his military calm.

'At the stroke of twelve, on the day of your wedded bliss, expect not a kiss... but the icy embrace of the abyss,' Lyn recited. Her words fell heavily in the silence. An involuntary shudder coursed through her body.

Ant lifted his gaze from his own card, mirroring Lyn's shock. He depicted the same haunting scene, but the message was different, yet equally menacing. "When the bells toll for thee, let the village be witness to what cannot be."

A cold draught filled the pub as if on cue, sending a chill through the hostelry. It was as though the very elements conspired to underscore the dread of the moment.

'Who would send such a horrible thing?' Lyn's sharp brain wrestled with the puzzle, even as her heart raced with foreboding. Her eyes, usually so full of resolve, now flickered with the flame of concern.

'Someone with a taste for the dramatic, or...' Ant's words trailed off, his thoughts unspoken yet hanging heavy between them. The easy-going laughter and banter of the Wherry Arms felt worlds away, replaced by a tangible concern that pressed in upon their shoulders.

'Or someone who means to do us harm,' Lyn finished for him, the gravity of the situation settling upon her like a mantle. The Earl and Countess Stanton had been nothing but supportive, enveloping them in the fabric of tradition and community. Yet here they were, the future Lord and Lady Stanton, targets of a threat that seemed ripped from the pages of a gothic novel.

'Let's not jump to conclusions.' Ant attempted to rally, though the effort seemed Herculean, as he tucked the invitation back into its envelope. 'We'll figure this out.'

'I hope so.' Lyn's voice was steely now, her determination clear. The envelope crinkled in her grip as if echoing her resolve.

Ant and Lyn sat in shock, regularly glancing at the poison post. The mystery that had landed in their laps promised a path that would lead them through imagined and real dangers in the coming days.

'Peter, we need you,' Lyn's voice was firm as she dialled their police friend's number, the urgency clear in her tone. Ant nodded his support from across the table.

'Trouble at t'mill?' came Peter Riley's joking response, a throwback to old detective serials they all enjoyed. But his levity quickly faded under the gravity of Lyn's voice.

'More like trouble with a capital 'T',' Lyn said. 'We've received an unsettling invitation...'

'Alright, give me half an hour.' There was the sound of rustling, a testament to Peter's readiness to leap into action, even after hours. 'I'll be with you soon.'

'Thank you, Peter.' Lyn ended the call, but her eyes stayed on the phone, as if willing it to bring them immediate answers.

Ant tried to chuckle; a hollow sound that got lost in the

pub's hubbub. 'That man could find a needle in a haystack even if the haystack was on fire.'

'Something tells me he'll need to be on form to sort this out for us,' Lyn replied, reaching out to squeeze Ant's hand. The touch meant to comfort, but Ant flinched, an involuntary reaction that didn't go unnoticed by Lyn.

'Hey, you, okay?' Her concern etched in the lines around her eyes.

'Fine,' Ant lied, trying to staple a smile onto his face. His gaze drifted to the window, where the wind played a mournful tune as it whirled around ancient structures. This was a tune he understood.

'Ant...' Lyn started, but he stood abruptly, the legs of the chair scraping against the stone floor like a distress signal.

'I need some air,' he murmured and pushed his way past the other patrons, their curious eyes tracking his retreat.

Outside, the clean Norfolk air hit his lungs, but it did little to ease the tightness in his chest. He leaned against the pub's red brick wall, the rough texture grounding him to the present. Somewhere in the mid-distance, a dog barked, a mundane sound that should have been reassuring.

'Damn it,' Ant whispered, pressing his palms against his eyelids. Memories he'd fought hard to contain chose this moment to surge forward—a cacophony of sounds and sights from days he wished remained forgotten.

'Deep breaths,' he coached himself, the words a mantra against the encroaching panic. 'In and out, just like Dr Thorndike taught you.'

'Talking to oneself now, are we?' The earl's voice, deep and steady, emerged from the shadows. Ant hadn't noticed his approach, but there he stood, a figure of unwavering support.

9

'Old habits,' Ant joked weakly, meeting his father's parental gaze.

'Let's walk a bit,' the earl suggested, offering his arm in a gesture that was both respectful and protective. Together, they paced slowly along the cobblestone path of High Street, the rhythm of their steps a gentle counterpoint to Ant's racing heart.

'What's up?' the Earl asked, his voice carrying his experience. 'Come on, get it off your chest. You know what happens when you keep things bottled up.'

Ant briefed his father on recent events, then made a heartfelt admission. 'I wish people didn't assume I'm the strong one,' Ant admitted, his humour failing to mask the truth of his words.

'Strength isn't about never falling down, Anthony,' the earl replied sagely. 'It's about who's there to help you up when you do.'

'Speaking of help, didn't you say the inspector will arrive soon? A good man, that one,' the earl said. 'And don't you worry, we'll sort this mess out before you can say 'wedding cake.''

'Here's hoping,' Ant responded, allowing a genuine smile to cross his features for the first time since opening the envelope.

'Come on, let's head back inside,' the earl urged gently. 'We can't have the groom catching a chill before the big day.'

'Nor the bride thinking I've bolted,' Ant added, finding humour despite the darkness that loomed over the wedding.

They returned to the pub, ready to confront whatever challenges lay ahead.

Ant's hand was a tremor as he fumbled with his pint of Fen Bodger Pale Ale. The glass had a life of its own, mirroring the ghosts of doubt that had taken residence in his mind since the envelopes arrived.

'Potential suspects?' Lyn mused aloud; her tone was deceptively casual as she leaned back in her chair. 'It could be anyone harbouring a grudge. Or someone who simply thrives on causing chaos.'

'Or perhaps someone with a vendetta against the Stanton's?' Ant suggested, his voice low. 'The wedding is the talk of the village.'

The earl, who had been quietly observing from his chair, gave a slow nod. 'We can't rule out the possibility that this is an attack on what the family represents. Loyalty to the village, to each other—'

'Exactly, Dad.' Ant's eyes were steely now, the initial shock giving way to resolve. 'We ought to find out who's behind this before they try to do more than just scare us.'

'Peter will have his work cut out,' Lyn added.

'Speaking of which—' The earl fell silent as the pub door opened, allowing a breeze to slip through the bar, carrying whispers of encroaching autumn.

Detective Inspector Peter Riley stepped into the pub, the understated authority in his stride belying the urgency of his visit. He cast a quick glance at the foursome before speaking. 'I got here as soon as I could. Let's see these invitations, then.'

'They're grim,' Lyn warned, passing the envelope with a steady hand.

Peter's eyes scanned the contents, his expression unreadable. 'We'll need to move quickly. Someone wants to throw a spanner into your plans, and we can't let them succeed.' His words carried a promise to solve the case.

'Thanks, Peter,' Ant said, gratitude warming his voice. 'We're counting on you.'

'It could be an insider,' mused Fitch, the village garage owner, his thickset frame making for a powerful presence.

'Or someone who feeds off old rivalries,' Lyn responded, her teacher's mind categorising and assessing. 'Someone who never forgave or forgot.'

'Let's not jump to conclusions,' Peter cautioned. 'We'll consider every angle. Just remember, conjecture won't solve this. Evidence will.'

'Time is of the essence, though,' the earl said, a touch of steel beneath his calm exterior. 'We must act swiftly to ensure the safety of these two, or indeed, anyone who might impede this obnoxious individual.'

'Agreed,' Peter affirmed. 'We have until the wedding to unravel this lot. My gut feeling is this is more than mischief. It carries all the hallmarks of malice.'

As the afternoon wore on, the small gathering felt the menace of an unseen adversary. Yet amidst the brewing storm, their unity was as unyielding as the ancient walls that sheltered them—walls that had withstood countless trials.

Ant drummed his fingers on the wooden table as a rhythmic counterpoint to Lyn's reassuring pat on his hand. 'We won't let some cowardly letters push us around,' she declared with a chin-up defiance that could rally an army— or at least a roomful of concerned villagers.

'Quite right,' Ant's father chimed in, his voice steady. 'The Stanton blood isn't known for cowering. We face storms head-on.'

'Speaking of which,' Peter Riley said, flashing a smile that was equal parts reassurance and mischief. 'We'll crack this before you can say 'I do.' Though I'd prefer not to have any unscheduled 'adventures' interrupting the nuptials.'

'Adventures?' Lyn quirked an eyebrow. 'Is that what we're calling threats these days?'

'Only the ones that come with RSVPs,' Peter replied, winking at her.

'Goodness, no sense in letting the blighters think they've got us rattled,' the earl said. 'Besides, Lyn would have my hide should my darling boy show up looking anything less than dapper on his wedding day.'

'True,' Lyn agreed, a playful glint in her eye. 'Can't have the groom outshone by the flower arrangements.'

'Or by Fitch's top hat,' the earl added dryly, eliciting chuckles all around.

'Let's not forget, there's more to this than bravado,' Peter interjected, leaning forward. 'This isn't just about being stoical; it's about keeping you two safe and catching whoever is behind this.'

'Which means we need a solid plan,' Lyn said, her voice taking on the commanding tone she used when organising school events. 'Peter, you'll chase down leads. Ant, you'll focus on keeping Stanton Hall running, so there are no hiccups for the wedding. And I'll make sure the community doesn't panic.'

'Teamwork,' Ant nodded.

'Right, then.' Peter stood, the transition from banter to action seamless. 'I'll have a chat with Jed. I'll get him to go over things again. It's amazing what people remember once they put their mind to it.'

Amidst pub chatter and howling wind, they echoed—a reminder of unwavering bonds.

Ant gave the heavy parchment of the invitation another look, the gold-embossed lettering mocking him with its twisted elegance. He attempted to chuckle, but it turned into a strangled gasp.

'Who'd have thought getting married would drop us into a plot thick enough for Agatha Christie herself?' Lyn jested.

'Modern-day England, where you expect rain on your wedding day, not... this.' Ant flicked the corner of the paper as if it would somehow make the words less ominous. 'An 'exclusive' event, they call it.'

'Exclusive as in 'by invitation only' rarely implies a threat,' Lyn replied dryly, her usual buoyant spirit dimmed by the unwanted invitation.

'Perhaps it's someone's idea of a sick joke?' Ant suggested. Lyn's demeanour illustrated she was far from convinced.

'Jokes are funny. This has the chill of the Phantom Coach of Potter Heigham,' she said, struggling against the tide of concern.

'Right. Ghosts, misty threats, and all we're missing is a hound baying,' Ant remarked, trying to lighten the mood. His attempt at humour seemed to dissipate like breath in the frigid air outside the Wherry Arms pub.

'Let's not borrow trouble from tomorrow,' Lyn responded. 'We've got Peter on it, and he's worth his weight in gold, or should that be in detective novels?'

'True. Though I wish some things stayed within the pages of books,' Ant conceded, stroking his chin thoughtfully. 'I'd rather deal with a bad-tempered flock of sheep any day.'

'Or unruly schoolchildren,' Lyn added, her mouth twitching upward. 'They're far less cryptic than whatever game this is.'

'Game or not, we won't let it spoil our day,' Ant said, the resolve in his voice steadier now. 'Dad's right about tradition and resilience.'

Ant glanced at the time on his mobile home screen, then stood. 'Let's head back to yours for an hour to do some thinking,' Ant suggested to Lyn. 'Then we'll have to get back to the Hall, because it won't prepare itself for our wedding.'

'Nor fend off mystery invitations,' Lyn quipped, rising to join him. They walked arm in arm, finding comfort in their shared experiences.

As they stepped outside, the wind howled around them with renewed vigour. It was as if nature itself was whispering of changes on the horizon, of ancient traditions and new vows entwined with questions that begged answers.

Chapter Two

TEA AND QUESTIONS

Wednesday, 3rd September: 4.00 pm

ANT AND LYN sat opposite each other at the worn pine kitchen table of the Old Schoolhouse, a bastion of stability in an otherwise uncertain afternoon. The air was still, and the dim light struggled to fully illuminate the puzzling scene before them. Two cream-coloured envelopes, each bearing their names in an elegant, sweeping script, spread out like a bad hand in a game of poker.

'Curious,' Lyn murmured, her normally light-hearted tone edged with unease. Her fingers hovered over the invitations but refrained from touching them, as though they might bite.

Ant reached for the invitation addressed to him. His hands betrayed a faint tremble that belied his calm facade. The manifestation did not escape Lyn's observant gaze.

'Ant, darling,' she said softly, concern etching her brow, 'Are you alright?'

'Of course,' Ant replied, though the tremor in his voice

suggested otherwise. He chuckled, but it was hollow, nothing like his usual warm baritone. 'Just the weather playing tricks on my nerves,' he lied, nodding towards the window where the leaves outside barely stirred.

'Antony Stanton, I know windblown leaves when I see them, and I know you.' Lyn's eyes locked onto his, her expression firm, yet filled with empathy. 'PTSD flaring up?'

'Perhaps a touch,' he admitted, setting the invitation down as if it weighed far more than paper should. 'But I'll manage, Lyn. I always do.'

'Managing isn't living,' she countered gently, reaching across to still his restless hands with her own. 'You don't have to go back to your military doctor if you're uncomfortable with him. What about Dr Thorndike? He was brilliant with you last time.'

'Dr Thorndike,' Ant repeated pensively, as if tasting the idea. 'Yes, I suppose I could... I'll think about it.'

'Don't just think, Ant,' Lyn said, squeezing his hands reassuringly. 'Promise me you won't just smile and soldier on.'

'Smile and carry on,' he mused, a ghost of his usual humour flickering in his eyes. 'Isn't that the English way?'

'Perhaps,' Lyn conceded, a playful glint in her own eye. 'But sometimes even the English must admit when it's time to ask for help.'

'Very well,' Ant replied. 'I promise I'll contact the doc.'

'Thank you,' Lyn said, her smile genuine as she released his hands. 'Now, let's figure out who sent these blasted invitations before whoever sent them gets too close. I'm having no one ruin my wedding day.'

Doggedly renewing their spirits, Ant, and Lyn leaned in, heads together, ready to face the tempest ahead.

Lyn's laughter was a gentle breeze through the tension

that hung in the kitchen, dispersing it like autumn leaves. 'Once we sort all this unpleasantness,' she said with a twinkle in her eye, 'We'll have our wedding, and then New Zealand awaits.'

'New Zealand?' Ant quirked an eyebrow, momentarily distracted from the ominous invitations. 'With its serene lakes and those towering mountains?'

'Exactly,' Lyn nodded, leaning back in her chair, her blond hair catching the late afternoon light. 'We can leave all this behind us. Remember, we're retiring from our amateur sleuthing, so when we get back, a new life lies ahead for us.'

'Retiring?' Ant snorted, picking at the edge of the invitation as if trying to peel away the mystery. 'Except for this last hurrah where some bonkers bloke is trying to see us off before we can cut the cake.'

'Stress-free, isn't it?' she chuckled, shaking her head.

A firm knock on the front door punctuated their shared moment of levity. They exchanged a glance, the warmth of their mirth replaced by uncertainty. Who could that be?

'Stay here,' Lyn murmured, a protective edge to her voice as she stood up, but Ant was already on his feet.

'Four fists are better than two if it's our mystery bloke,' he replied, his tone light but resolute. Together, they navigated the narrow hallway toward answers that awaited them beyond the heavy wooden door.

Ant's hand brushed Lyn's as he reached for the Yale lock, a silent pulse of understanding passing between them. The door swung open to reveal Detective Inspector Peter Riley, his familiar face creased with ill-disguised concern.

'Peter!' Lyn exclaimed; her voice threaded with palpable relief. 'Thank goodness it's you.'

'Come in, come in,' Ant said, stepping aside, an

unspoken understanding warming his eyes as they met Peter's.

'Sorry to drop by unannounced,' Peter began, his tone apologetic, but the urgency in his movements belied any genuine regret as he crossed the threshold. He slipped off his coat, hanging it on the aged brass hook by the door—a minor act that echoed countless visits before.

'Unannounced is the least of our worries,' Lyn replied, leading the way to the kitchen.

Their steps were brisk, a counterpoint to the drone of the kettle beginning its chorus anew. The kitchen, usually a bastion of hearty meals and laughter, now held a taut silence, the air charged with a sense of foreboding.

Peter entered the kitchen, taking in the scene—the invitations on the table, Ant's trembling hands, inviting him to join their council.

'Looks like I've stumbled into a tempest,' Peter said, settling into the seat with the ease of a seasoned officer.

'More like a hurricane,' Ant quipped, attempting to slice through the tension with a hint of humour. 'But not the kind you can track on a weather map.'

'Indeed,' Peter acknowledged, his deep-set eyes reflecting a well of determination. 'Let's see if we can't make sense of this latest gust.'

In the cosy confines of Lyn's kitchen, with the wind whispering secrets to the windowpanes and the steadfast presence of their trusted friend, Ant, and Lyn felt the flicker of hope. Together, they would withstand this tempest.

'Peter, we've been over it a thousand times,' Lyn said, the skin around her eyes tightened with concern. 'It's as if our wedding guest list has sprouted fangs overnight.'

'Spot on,' Ant added, his voice steady but his fingers betraying a serious health problem as they rested unsteadily on the tabletop. 'Someone knows about Saturday, and they're not sending well-wishes.'

'Curious that they should choose now to strike,' Peter mused, steepling his fingers beneath his chin. 'A time of celebration turned into something... ominous.'

'Whoever it is,' Lyn pressed on, 'they've done their homework on us.

'Quite the puzzle,' Peter conceded, his mouth tipping downward slightly. 'But I assure you both—'

He paused, locking eyes with them, his commitment tangible.

'—I'll do everything within my power to unravel the mystery. Protecting you is more than duty; it's a promise. Speaking of which,' he continued, leaning forward slightly, 'We've canvassed the area for that young lad Jed chanced upon. And the landlord's memory proved sharper than we thought. Gave us a few threads to pull at.'

'Jed's a sharp one,' Ant acknowledged with a smile, the lines of worry around his eyes softening. 'I've always said he'd make a better detective than half the blokes down at the station.'

Peter agreed, his lips twitching upwards. 'Let's hope those threads lead us somewhere less tangled than Phyllis's latest yarns about the earl's rose bushes.'

'Or her theories on global warming,' Lyn chimed in, the tension easing from her shoulders as she shared a conspiratorial grin with the two men.

Peter chuckled. 'Now, let's get started on untangling this knot before it tightens any further. Time and tide and all that.'

Ant's hand rested on his invitation, his fingers tracing the embossed lettering again, as if he could draw out the sender's identity through touch. Lyn reached across the table, her hand covering his—a silent sign of togetherness in their shared turmoil. Ant acknowledged his fiance's loving gesture. Then he turned his attention back to the envelope. 'I don't recognise the cypher. It doesn't belong to any of the families we know of. I spent hours in the archive room at the Hall. Nothing in Debrett's, or any of the other reference books I looked up. This must just be a made-up design that purports to represent...and forgive me for sounding pompous, a noble family.'

Peter inspected the coat of arms on the wax seal, broken in two, when Ant and Lyn opened the envelopes. 'I'm happy to believe what you say. You move around in these circles, I don't.'

Peter's comment didn't take a rise out of Ant. His comment was born of a well-established friendship with the pair.

'Peter,' Ant began, his voice steady with an undercurrent of emotion, 'we can't thank you enough. Having you—'

'With us,' Lyn concluded. Her gaze meeting Riley's with a depth of trust that was earned over countless investigations and social contact.

'Stop it, you'll have me blushing next,' Peter replied. 'You've got my word on it. I'm in this with you to the end.'

'Thank goodness,' Lyn said with a half-smile. 'We're rather fond of having you around, especially when there's a rogue element trying to spoil the happiest day of our lives.'

'Rogue element seems about right,' Ant mused, leaning back in his chair. 'But who? That's the million-pound question, isn't it?'

'Indeed.' Peter pulled out a small leather-bound notepad from his jacket pocket, flipping it open with a practised motion. 'Now, let's hash this out. Any ideas who could be behind this? Old grudges, perhaps? Or someone with a vendetta against you getting married?'

'Could be anyone with a bone to pick,' Lyn said, tapping a finger against her chin. 'Remember Ian Lister? The disgraced Police Commander? He's always had it in for us since we had him put away for trying to set someone else up for a crime he committed.'

'Desperation leads people to dramatic measures,' Peter pointed out, scribbling notes. 'When I worked for him in Kent, he could be incredibly kind to his staff. Then, without warning, he'd change into something resembling a tyrant. You remember how he treated me when he came here to take over the investigation I'd begun? He was determined to have his way. Ruthless, some might say.'

'Then there's Phyllis,' Lyn suggested, albeit hesitantly. 'I know, from the sublime to the ridiculous. She's been quite vocal about the 'decline of traditional village values.' Maybe she sees our modern take on the wedding as a step too far?'

'Phyllis?' Ant chuckled, despite the seriousness of the conversation. 'I doubt she'd go beyond tutting disapprovingly over her garden fence, while ordering her mate, Betty, to carry on digging the flower beds.'

'Still,' Peter interjected, 'no stone unturned, right? We'll investigate Lister and monitor Phyllis, just in case.'

'Speaking of stones,' Ant added, 'What about Roger Arbuthnot? He's been acting odd lately. Though I can't imagine him being involved in something so sordid.'

'He's harmless,' Lyn countered. 'And he adores you, Ant. He wouldn't jeopardise the wedding.'

'Hm...I suppose you're right. This sort of things makes you jump at shadows,' Ant conceded with a sigh. 'I guess we should also consider the possibility of an outsider, someone not tied to the village's way of doing things.'

Lyn giggled, 'What? You mean like murder?'

'You've been watching too much Midsomer Murder on the telly,' Ant replied, thankful for a moment of mirth.

'An interloper amidst our tight-knit community,' Peter said thoughtfully, closing his notepad with a snap. 'A modern-day marauder clashing with the old-world charm of our hamlet.'

'You've got it,' Lyn said, a determined glint in her eye. 'We find this person, and we ensure the wedding goes ahead without a hitch,' Lyn replied.

'Gotcha,' Ant replied.

'Then it's settled,' Peter concluded. First, we'll review Jed's statement, then check if Lister knows any of the people he's associated with. Finally, we'll monitor the activity in the village. Nothing escapes the collective gaze of our residents for long.'

'Let's hope not,' Lyn said, rising from her seat. 'Because come Saturday, rain, or shine, wind or calm, we're getting married.'

'You've said that once already,' Ant teased.

'And I'll keep saying it until you say, 'I do', and we both get out of that church in one piece.'

A moment of silence followed as the conversation fizzled out. Ant leaned back in his chair and rubbed at his temples, a familiar haze of unease clouding his thoughts. The kitchen, with its warm hues and the comforting scent of Lyn's baking, suddenly felt as confining as a military bunker. He glanced at Detective Inspector Peter Riley, perched on the edge of the table, his detective's mind whirring.

'Peter,' Ant began, his voice carrying the slight tremor of the calm before a storm. 'I must admit, this situation is bringing up some old memories that are unsettling me.'

'Your PTSD?' Peter asked, his tone gentle as a breeze but sharp enough to cut to chase.

Ant lowered his gaze to the tiled floor, but forced a half-smile that didn't quite work. 'It's like being back on active service without sand and heat.' He let out a dry chuckle that sounded more like rustling parchment than mirth.

'Ant, I've seen you handle more pressure than this,' Peter said, getting up to place a reassuring hand on his friend's shoulder. 'You're not alone in this. We're here for you.'

'Thanks, Peter,' Ant replied, nodding. His gaze shifted to Lyn, who had been quietly observing the exchange, her expression one of total support and understanding.

'Besides,' Lyn interjected, 'you promised me you'd take better care of yourself. No more 'stiff upper lip' antics, okay? Dr Thorndike said—'

'I know what he said,' Ant interrupted, a mock grumble colouring his words, while he avoided her knowing look. 'And I'm not exactly chuffed about needing help, but I'll do it. For us.'

'Good,' Lyn said firmly, the resolve in her voice as steadfast as the ancient oak in the village square. 'Because we're not letting some twisted plotter steal our joy. Not now, never.'

'That's the spirit,' Peter agreed with a nod, his demeanour echoing the comment. 'We'll tackle this together, one step at a time. Just remember, Ant. It will pass.'

'I know,' Ant mused. 'Right, some steps. I'll add that to the wedding list. Between 'pick up suit' and 'avoid being murdered' there should be time to do it.'

Lyn rolled her eyes affectionately, and even Peter allowed himself a small smile at Ant's attempt to lighten the mood.

'Seriously though, take your moments,' Peter said. 'Solitude can be a sanctuary, even amid chaos - just don't take the 'I want to be alone' stuff too far. You know that's not good for you, either.'

'Sanctuary...' Ant repeated softly, a glimmer of gratitude flickering in his eyes. 'I'll keep that in mind.'

'Great job,' Peter said, patting Ant on the back. 'Now, let's see if we can't put a stop to this nonsense before you two lovebirds tie the knot, shall we?'

'Before the knot becomes a noose, preferably,' Lyn quipped, the light-heartedness in her voice belying the steel in her character.

'Preferably,' Ant echoed, feeling a little lighter, a little readier to face the winds of uncertainty—with his fiance and his friend solidly at his side.

Ant tucked the invitations into a drawer, a symbolic gesture that they were putting aside their bewilderment to focus on action. 'So,' he said confidently, 'We begin with what we know, which is as uncertain as next week's weather forecast—likely unpleasant.'

'First,' Lyn said, rolling up her sleeves as if preparing for a physical skirmish, 'we gather our resources. I've got the school staff who are eyes and ears all over the village. Gossip flows through those halls faster than tea through a strainer.'

'Good,' Peter nodded, writing notes into his police pad with the speed of a man used to multitasking under pressure. 'I'll rally the nearby constabularies to keep an eye out for anything unusual, especially lone individuals doing stuff that seems odd.'

'Speaking of which,' Ant chimed in, 'Dad's gathering the Hall's security footage. Might be worth a gander, see if our mystery guest made a cameo appearance.'

'Brilliant,' Lyn said, her brain ticking over like a well-oiled clock. 'And I'll put a word out discreetly. Someone might have seen something that could lead us to our would-be saboteur.'

'Discreet being the operative word,' Peter cautioned. He met her gaze with an earnestness that underscored the gravity beneath his calm exterior.

'Of course,' she replied, her manner suggesting that discretion was her middle name. 'We don't want to spook them. Just... nudge them into the light.'

The trio sat back momentarily to consider their strategy. The kitchen, once a place of domestic tranquillity, had transformed into their command centre. Intricate tactics against an unseen foe now replaced domestic chores.

'Right then,' Ant said, pushing back his chair and standing up with a purposeful air. 'Let's get to it.'

'Agreed,' Peter confirmed, pocketing his mobile and rising to match Ant's resolve. 'I'll start making calls the moment I get to the Station.'

Lyn followed suit; her demeanour was resolute. 'And I'll chat with the staff this afternoon. Most of them will have stayed back to prepare for a teaching inspection. We might just find a chink in our adversary's armour.'

'May the best sleuths win,' Lyn declared, her smile fierce and confident.

Ant concurred, feeling his earlier fears dissipate like fog in the morning sun. 'To victory, then. And matrimony, in whichever order they come.'

'Preferably before the 'I dos',' Peter quipped, opening the front door to depart.

'Or the 'I don'ts,'' Ant added, winking.

With a shared chuckle, they parted ways—their spirits buoyed by the plan they'd crafted and the knowledge that, come rain or shine, they were in this together.

Chapter Three

A HESITANT WITNESS

Wednesday, 3rd September: 6.00 pm

ANT STOOD ALONE on the edge of the manicured lawn at Stanton Hall, his hands buried deep in the pockets of his tweed jacket. The gentle rustle of leaves whispered secrets only he seemed privy to, but their words were not of comfort. He watched with a distant gaze as white garlands and silk ribbons adorned the ancient oak in readiness for their wedding reception. Each bloom added weight to the armour of memories he carried.

'Everything alright, Ant?' Lyn's voice cut through the stillness, light as the breeze yet carrying the strength of her resolve.

He smiled weakly, a facade that crumbled as quickly as it had formed. 'Just... thinking,' he murmured, his heavy eyes betraying another sleepless night.

'About what?' she pressed gently, though her intuition already mapped the contours of his heartache.

'Us, the wedding, keeping you safe...' His voice trailed

off, a haunted look taking hold as he stared into the distance. Anxiety gnawed at him—a relentless storm that no amount of planning could quell. Protecting Lyn from the unseen threats that loomed over their joyous occasion was a task he bore alone, or so he believed.

'Ant, I—'

But he was already yards away. It was not the first time Ant had vanished into the shadowed corners of his mind, seeking refuge in solitude when the cacophony of stress became too much.

Lyn sighed, her breath forming a misty cloud in the early evening air. She knew this dance well—the ebb and flow of Ant's presence—and understood that he needed these moments. Alone, he found his bearings, and she respected the silent pact they shared. He would always return to her side, no matter how far the demons chased him into the recesses of his own psyche.

'Take your time, my love,' she whispered to the emptiness he left behind, her voice infused with a tenderness that only true understanding could foster.

The sun peeked out from behind a cloud, its rays glinting off the windows of the stately home, promising warmth and the reassurance of continuity. Lyn turned to the wedding preparations, her hands moving deftly among the flowers, each petal a testament to her unwavering focus. She knew the Earl of Stanton would oversee the search for Ant to ensure his son was safe and sound.

———

Wednesday 3rd September: 6.00 pm

THE DOOR to the modest brick house swung open, and Peter stared down at a pair of wide-eyed parents. He tipped his hat, the very picture of rural constabulary politeness.

'Evening, Mr. Harper, Mrs Harper. I'm here to have a quick word with young Timmy about a small matter down at The Wherry Arms.'

The Harpers exchanged a glance that spoke volumes of parental dread before beckoning him inside. With his parent's permission, Peter sauntered through to the kitchen to find Timmy sat at a table wearing a guilty look.

'Timmy, lad,' Peter began, keeping his voice even and reassuring, 'You're not in trouble. But I need to talk about those invitations you dropped off at the pub.'

The boy's shoulders visibly relaxed, but his eyes darted to his mother, who stood arms folded, her expression a blend of relief and admonishment.

'An old bloke,' Timmy began. 'He gave me ten quid to take 'em there.' His cheeks reddened under his mother's sharp gaze. 'Sorry, Mum.'

'Old bloke?' Peter prodded gently, jotting notes in his pocketbook.

'Big raincoat, flat cap,' Timmy mumbled. 'Glasses. Didn't smile, not once.'

'Did you see where this man went after he spoke to you?'

'Didn't stick around to watch him, did I?' Timmy said with a flash of youthful exasperation. 'Grabbed the money and legged it to the pub, didn't I?'

'Of course, of course,' Peter chuckled, closing his pocketbook. 'Thank you, Timmy. You've been an immense help.'

After thanking the boy's parents and reassuring them their son had helped his investigation, Peter made his way to the police station.

The detective surveyed his team with a sense of urgency that belied his calm demeanour. The map on the wall, dotted with pins, looked like a modern art piece dedicated to village life.

'Listen up,' he announced. 'Our person of interest is likely still local. Given the sightings in two locations within the village, he won't stray far. I want every bed-and-breakfast, every Airbnb checked within a five-mile radius. Pubs too, any that offer a bed for the night.'

He planted a firm finger on Stanton Hall, positioned central on the map. 'We must find this man, and soon.'

'Shouldn't be too hard,' quipped Sergeant Riley. 'Sounds like half the retired blokes on a wet Wednesday, Guv.'

Peter allowed himself a thin smile. This was their patch, and whatever the cost, they'd keep it safe.

———

Wednesday, 3rd September: 7.30 pm

THE SCENT of lilies and chrysanthemums filled the air as Lyn Blackthorn carefully adjusted a garland on a pew in the village church. Her hands were steady, betraying none of the turmoil that had been swirling around the upcoming wedding. She turned at the sound of footsteps echoing against the stone floor, her light blue eyes meeting Peter's with an expectant calm.

'Still at it? It's been a long day for you, that's for sure,' the detective said as he surveyed the floral arrangements. 'Where's Anthony?'

Lyn's shoulders sank. 'At school, I call it time out.'

'His PTSD?'

She nodded. 'He'll be back when he's ready. Until then, it's better I keep myself busy. Any news for me?'

Peter nodded. 'We're doing a sweep of the local B&Bs and guesthouses. Also, I'm arranging for the church, Stanton Hall, and your place to be under a twenty-four-hour watch. Just as a precaution.'

'Thank's, Peter,' Lyn replied, her gratitude genuine, knowing well the web of safety he was weaving around them.

As they spoke, Reverend Morton shuffled into the church, his face a pale canvas of shock upon hearing snippets of their conversation. 'A plotter, here? In our peaceful haven?' he gasped, the very thought sending a tremor through his timeworn frame.

'Reverend,' Peter asked, turning to face the cleric, 'Have you noticed any unfamiliar faces recently? Anyone who might have seemed out of place?'

At first, the Reverend shook his head, his mind wading through the many faces that sought solace within the ancient walls. Then a memory surfaced. 'Well, there was this one chap last Monday. Seemed lost in thought, or rather, troubled.'

'Can you describe him?' Peter pressed, sensing the tingle of a lead unfurling before them.

'Middle-aged, spectacled, wearing a heavy coat despite the mildness of the day. He didn't smile, nor did he respond when I offered a word.'

'Sounds like our man,' Peter murmured, exchanging a glance with Lyn. 'Was he taking an unusual interest in the church?'

'I couldn't say,' the reverend admitted.

Lyn's lips pressed together, steel entering her voice. 'This is too real, Peter. It's not just pranks anymore.'

'Hey now,' Peter said softly, placing a reassuring hand on her shoulder. 'We've got it under control. This is still your day, and nothing's going to spoil it.'

Outside, the wind whispered through the yew trees in the churchyard, a reminder of the unseen forces that played at the edges of tradition. Inside, the fragrance of flowers mingled doggedly with a touch of defiance.

———

Wednesday 3rd September: 10.00 pm

PETER STOOD at the last bed-and-breakfast. The cottage with a thatched roof had roses climbing around the door, giving it a calm vibe despite the village's troubles. The landlady, a sprightly woman in her late seventies with a penchant for floral dresses, shook her head.

'What time do you call this?' the elderly lady said as she chastised the detective for call so late.

'I'm sorry,' Peter began as he stood before the half-open door. 'It is urgent, I assure you. You see, I'm looking for a man in connection with a serious incident, and wondered if you'd come across any strangers over the last few days?' He regretted the way he'd framed his question immediately.'

'Strangers? You are aware I run a Bed & Breakfast establishment, which, I take it, is why you're here? Anyway, to answer your silly question, the only people I've seen lately are the usual batch of birdwatchers. All binoculars-and-khaki-shorts. They all camp these days, so they're no use to me, cheapskates.'

'Oh, er, I see,' Peter replied. 'Well, thank you for your time, and, again, please accept my apologies for the late call.'

She peered over her glasses, scrutinising Peter as though he were a rare species of titmouse. 'Is there trouble brewing., then?'

'Routine check, Mrs. Potts,' Peter replied, maintaining the facade of casual diligence. 'Just checking.'

'More like chasing geese if you ask me,' she huffed, sending him on his way with a flap of her hand.

As Peter walked to his car, the wind picked up, tossing leaves into a frenetic dance across the cobbled lane. He let out a sigh, watching the spirals of foliage mimic his own circular thoughts. False leads and dead ends had been the anthem of the day, and the elusive 'old bloke' remained a spectre at the periphery of the upcoming festivities.

'Chasing geese indeed,' he muttered, sliding behind the wheel. The car's dashboard blinked at him with the time, reminding him that the wedding was drawing closer with every tick. Frustration gnawed at him, but he pushed it down with the same determination that had seen him through countless other cases.

'Right then, you old ghost,' he addressed the invisible adversary, 'You can run, but you can't hide. Not from me.'

Peter pulled out his mobile and dialled his second-in-command. 'Sergeant Bell? It's me. I want another sweep done—every inn, every public house, even the blasted campsites. And get me the CCTV footage from the scrapyard, the pub, anywhere our man might have passed through.'

'Another sweep, Gov?' came the weary voice over the line, tinged with the fatigue of a man who'd already trudged through half the county. 'That's a tall order this late in the day.'

'Then we best get started,' Peter said firmly, cutting off any room for protest. 'This isn't some merry jaunt in the countryside, and I'll be damned if I let some rain coated rascal ruin the auspicious event on Saturday.'

'Understood, Guv,' Sergeant Bell replied, the resolve in his tone matching Peter's own. 'We'll turn this place upside down if we have to.'

'Good man,' Peter said, disconnecting the call. He glanced up at the sky, where the moon fought a valiant battle against gathering clouds—a metaphor not lost on him.

———

Thursday, 4th September: 8.45 am

LYN, still surrounded by colourful flowers, consulted the list in her hand as she directed the florists with a keen eye. The smell of fresh earth and blooms filled the Great Hall, a fragrance that whispered of new beginnings and age-old promises. She tucked a wayward strand of blond hair behind her ear, then turned as the heavy oak door creaked open.

'Sleep well?' she asked, watching Detective Inspector Peter Riley step inside.

Not really,' Peter grumbled, though his eyes twinkled with the dogged determination of a man not easily thwarted by dead ends and false leads. 'Is Anthony back yet?'

'Still missing in action, but it shouldn't be long now. His dad is out looking for him, you know, visiting the places he often goes to when he has an episode. In the meantime, pleased to take my mind off a wayward fiance and uncooperative flowers.' Lyn offered a hard-won smile.

'I've got just the tonic. Let's compare notes to see where we're up with the mystery man, shall we?'

The pair retreated to a corner of the voluminous space, the stone walls around them echoing with the hushed footsteps of staff and the rustle of foliage being arranged. Lyn unfolded a map of the village across an octagonal table.

'Here's where the lad said he saw the old bloke,' Peter pointed, tapping on the scrapyard just on the village outskirts. 'And here's the Wherry Arms.' His finger traced a route between the two points. Then there's the odd fellow at the church.' Peter hesitated, rubbing his chin thoughtfully. 'The reverend was quite certain about the coat and glasses.'

'Right,' Lyn agreed, her lips pursed. 'And it's the same description from the young lad. There must be a connection.'

'Has to be,' Peter echoed, frowning. He leaned closer to the map, his gaze sharp. 'What we need is something that ties him to—'

'Wait,' Lyn interrupted, her voice suddenly charged with excitement. 'The raincoat and glasses, yes, but what was he doing there? You know, walking around, taking pictures?'

'Just the opposite, in fact. The reverend said the man seemed troubled.'

'Troubled how?' replied Lyn, her interest piqued.

'Like he was grappling with some internal storm. And that got me thinking about the weather.'

'Weather?'

'Yes, Lyn. It's been warm, almost hot lately. Why wear such a heavy coat unless you needed the pockets?'

'Pockets for what?' Lyn frowned.

'Exactly, for what?'

Lyn's face lit up with realisation. 'What if he was hiding something? Something relevant to the wedding?'

'Or to disrupt it,' Peter added, the pieces clicking into place. 'We've been looking for someone acting suspiciously. Perhaps he's using the hustle of your wedding preparations as cover?'

'Which means he could've planted something already,' Lyn's eyes widened, a chill running down her spine despite the warmth of the church.

'Right under our noses,' Peter acknowledged grimly. 'Clever, using the confusion to his advantage, but not clever enough. We'll sweep every inch of the church and keep an eye out for anything that doesn't fit.'

'Or anyone who's dressed at odds with the weather,' Lyn quipped.

'If he used the coat to hide planting something in the church, he'll have ditched that now to better blend in. Anyway, let's hope our suspect isn't as seasoned in this game as he believes,' Peter said, his gaze firm. 'Because the only storm he'll be causing is the one we'll bring down on him.'

'Then let's get to it, Detective,' Lyn said, rolling up the map with a determined snap. 'Before the next gust of wind blows more trouble our way.'

———

Thursday 4th September: 11.15 pm

LYN STOOD in the grand foyer of Stanton Hall, admiring the intricate stonework with awe and deep contemplation. The breakthrough, in the case, energised her and made her feel closer to solving the mystery.

'Ant will like the progress we've made,' she muttered, stroking the pendant that lay close to her heart—a token of their shared history and forthcoming future.

'Love what?' came a voice from the doorway, weary but unmistakably familiar.

Lyn spun around, her heart leaping at the sight of Ant, standing there like an anchor amidst the sea of chaos that threatened to engulf them both. His shoulders slumped, a testament to the invisible weight he bore, yet his presence was a balm to her frayed nerves.

'Ant!' She rushed forward, closing the gap with a few brisk steps and wrapped him in an embrace that spoke volumes more than words ever could.

In the background, his father watched the splendid scene. Job done in finding his son, the earl slipped out of sight, leaving Ant and Lyn to reunite.

'Sorry I took off,' he whispered into her hair. 'It all got too much. But I'm back now. I'm not going anywhere from now on.'

Pulling back slightly, Lyn studied his face—those lines of tension that seemed etched a little deeper, the shadows beneath his eyes a touch darker. Yet, there was a resolve in his gaze that matched her own.

'Promise me something?' she asked, her voice laced with equal parts concern and affection.

'I know what you're going to say. I promise, I'll make an appointment with Dr Thorndike to put a treatment plan in place—and stick to it this time. 'We can't have you shouldering this burden alone, especially not with...' His sentence faded away, but the implication lingered between them.

'Good,' said Lyn... 'But don't leave it too long.'

A few minutes passed as they enjoyed each other's company without the need to speak a word. In a far field, sheep grazed in the lush pasture of the Estate. Beyond the livestock, late summer tourists took advantage of the warm weather sailing on Stanton Broad.

'Now, what's been going on?' Ant said, gazing at his fiance. 'I heard about the fellow in the raincoat.'

'How?' Lyn asked.

'Reverend Morton. I called in, expecting to find you there.'

Lyn chuckled, despite the serious situation. 'Yes, our would-be saboteur has a flair for the dramatic. But Peter and I are on it. We've got the scent and we're not letting go.'

'Like a pair of bloodhounds,' Ant quipped, a grin tugging at the corner of his lips.

'Exactly,' Lyn agreed, her laughter mingling with his. 'And soon, we'll have this plotter wishing he'd chosen a sunnier disposition.'

They stood together, in the embrace of Stanton Hall's timeless facade, united in purpose and bound by the steadfast thread of devotion. Together, they were a force to be reckoned with.

'Alright then,' Lyn said, rolling her shoulders back in a display of readiness. 'Time to chase down a ghost before he acts out his demented RSVP plot.'

Ant gave her hand a gentle squeeze. 'We'll catch him. Fitch is going to give his wedding speech at our reception, whether he likes it!'

As Ant turned to make for the morning room with Lyn, the dulcet tone of the grandfather clock in the spacious reception area marked the hour. Its chime spoke of an ominous portent. It was a stark reminder that time, much like their mysterious adversary, would not wait.

As they settled into the deep leather sofas in the morning room, Lyn exhaled slowly, allowing herself a moment of vulnerability. She glanced at the aged portraits adorning the walls, their subjects' eyes seeming to follow her with silent, knowing stares. It was as if the very essence of Stanton Hall urged her to dig deeper.

Her mobile vibrated so that it skipped along the polished surface of a small mahogany side table. Retrieving the device, she saw Peter's name flash on the screen. Her heart skipped a beat.

'Peter. News?' she asked, bracing herself.

'Hi, Lyn. I'm afraid I've got a puzzle here.' Peter's voice crackled over the line, betraying an undercurrent of urgency.

'Go on,' she urged.

'It's Phyllis—she's certain she saw someone fitting our man's description entering the bakery early this morning. But when we arrived...' Peter paused; Lyn could picture his brow furrowing in consternation.

'Spit it out, Peter.'

'There baker said he's had no one in matching the description I gave. It makes me think Phyllis picked up a morsel of information from a villager. I imagine she then embellished the gossip to make it fit what she thinks she saw.'

Lyn's mind raced. If their suspect had been there, it meant he knew the village well—too well. But how could he enter without leaving a trace?

'Could Phyllis be correct?' Lyn asked.

'Maybe he didn't have that long coat on. But something doesn't sit right. We're going to keep looking, but this feels like... well, like trying to catch bubbles on the breeze.'

'Then we must change tactics,' Lyn decided, her eyes scanning Ant's concerned features.

'Indeed. But there's more,' Peter added. Lyn felt her pulse quicken. 'I've had a call from Jed about a stranger asking questions at the pub. Described him as middle-aged, wearing a raincoat, glasses, the lot.'

'It's got to be him,' Lyn announced.

'Exactly,' Peter replied. 'It could be nothing, or it could be the break we need. I'm heading there now.'

'Keep me updated,' Lyn said, her mind already ticking through possibilities.

'Of course. Stay sharp, Lyn. Oh, and by the way. The vicar tells me Anthony has returned. Is he feeling any better?'

Lyn looked at her future husband and smiled. 'Yes, he's here. Do you want a word?'

Ant moved his hand towards the mobile.

'No, just tell him to get a good night's sleep and take it easy. He's got a busy few days coming up, and I don't just mean catching our man.'

Ant retracted his hand as he overheard Peter. The beginnings of a smile replaced his frown.

Lyn clicked the keypad to end the call and placed her mobile back on the side table. Just then, from the corner of her eye, she sensed movement outside the window—a mirage that danced just beyond the reach of the garden.

Her heart hammered as she approached the distorting glass panes of the enormous bay window. There, weaving through the statues and topiaries, was a figure cloaked in a long coat, moving with purpose toward a line of trees.

'Got you,' Lyn whispered, a triumphant smile curling her lips despite the chill that coursed through her veins.

She dashed out the door, leaving Ant in her trail. Lyn was determined to confront the enigma head-on. As she slipped into the brisk air. The wind had picked up, carrying with it the sense of unease.

Chapter Four

WISE HEADS

Thursday, 4th September: 2.30 pm

AMONG THE PAPERS on his office desk, Peter Riley felt an unusual sense of anxiety building up. The wedding was happening in just two days, and the person who sent the creepy invitation was still a mystery, making him feel uneasy. 'Blimey,' he muttered, and scrubbing a hand through his hair in vexed frustration, 'If this chap were any more slippery, he'd be a bar of soap in a public shower.'

The clock on the wall ticked remorselessly, each second resonating like the irritated tap of an impatient foot as Saturday approached. Peter had a nasty feeling the case was slipping away from him.

'Enough is enough,' Peter declared to the empty room. He knew what he had to do. His mentor beckoned.

The Norfolk landscape remained breathtaking as Peter approached the chocolate-box cottage. The interior of retired Chief Inspector Samuel Thompson's home testified to a life dedicated to unravelling mysteries. Now Peter stood to benefit from his mentor's wisdom.

'Sam,' Peter said, stepping into the warmth that always seemed to radiate from his mentor. Samuel Thompson owned an eagle-eyed gaze softened by laugh lines. His beard had a life of its own. Below, a smile lurked as comforting as a hot cuppa on a damp English morning.

'Peter, my boy!' Thompson's voice was rich in the timbre of experience. 'What brings you to my humble corner of Norfolk? Oh, let me guess—tied up in knots with the case?'

'Got it in one,' Peter admitted, sinking into the armchair that had become his confessional. Their relationship transcended the professional; Mutual respect and trust, forged in the fire of shared cases and the camaraderie that comes with knowing your back's covered.

'Whenever I hit a brick wall, I think about what you'd do,' Peter confessed, his words carrying the sincerity of his esteem for the retired detective. 'And right now, that wall is closing in mighty fast.'

'Ah, remember the Pennington affair?' Thompson reminisced, his eyes twinkling with the memory of a case long past. 'When we thought we were at a dead-end, and then—pop!—the answer was hiding in plain sight.'

'Pop indeed,' Peter chuckled, the tension easing from his shoulders a little. 'I could use one of those moments right about now.'

'Let's have a look, then,' Thompson said, gesturing toward the files Peter had brought with him. 'We'll crack this together, just like old times.'

As they delved into the details of the case, the creaking of the cottage's old timbers carried whispers of encouragement. In the comfortable confines of camaraderie and the interplay of wit and wisdom, Peter Riley found a renewed sense of purpose. Together, they would banish the clouds looming over the Stanton wedding.

The study was an oasis of wisdom where time seemed respectful enough to tread lightly. Chief Inspector Samuel Thompson's domain featured honey-oak shelves that cradled the weight of decades. His hand-written memoir stood proud among the leather-bound classics, symbolising the solved cases and captivating tales. The room was awash in the golden glow of a brass desk lamp, casting a halo over photos and trinkets from forgotten victories. A vintage type-writer rested on a side table. Its keys remained silent but poised, as if waiting for the next chapter of intrigue to unfold.

'Can't shake the feeling, Sam,' Peter began, perching uneasily on the edge of a plush armchair, like a bird too eager to nest. 'It's as though the answer's dancing just out of reach, taunting me.'

'Ah, the elusive last puzzle piece,' Thompson said, peering at Peter over the rim of his reading glasses. 'It enjoys a jest at our expense, doesn't it?'

'Right now, it's about as amusing as a whoopee cushion at a funeral,' Peter replied, his frustration clear. He tousled his hair, which mimicked the disarray of the papers scattered across Thompson's desk.

'Your issue is one of time. A luxury you can't afford,' he said, tapping a finger on the mahogany surface for emphasis. 'The wedding is, what, forty-eight hours away, and there's a snake lurking in the grass. You must find it before it strikes.'

Peter nodded. 'Sam, I'll turn over every stone if I have to,' Peter said.

'Stones, pebbles, or boulders, lad.' Thompson leaned back, his chair creaking under the shift. 'Just ensure you don't leave any unturned. Now, let's talk about suspects and motives. Remember, the devil loves to dance in the details. Now, let me see,' Thompson murmured, pushing aside a stack of books on botanical poisons. 'You've got a wedding hanging in the balance, a village on tenterhooks, and a culprit as slippery as an eel at a grease festival.'

'You might say so,' Peter sighed, his eyes scanning the room as if the walls themselves might divulge a clue. 'Every lead's turned into a blind alley.'

'Then perhaps you're sifting for gold in the wrong stream,' Thompson suggested, his voice carrying the tune of experience like an aged violin. 'Remember the Hastings debacle? The solution wasn't in the what or the who, but in the why.'

'Right, the why...' Peter echoed, his brow furrowing as he contemplated this angle. 'But the motive seems as cloudy as a British summer. The not so happy couple can't think of anyone. No one with a reason to halt the nuptials, let alone send threats of serious harm.'

'Interesting, eh?' Thompson chuckled softly. 'Sometimes, my boy, you need to look not at the clouds, but at where they cast their shadows.' He reached for a porcelain paperweight, shaped like Sherlock Holmes' iconic deerstalker hat, and gave it a tap. 'Cast your gaze where the light doesn't quite reach, and you might find your villain lurking.'

'Shadows,' Peter repeated, mulling over the words.

'Years of squinting at fine print and even finer alibis, my dear Riley,' Thompson quipped, his eyes crinkling at the edges.

Peter began scribbling as Thompson outlined several theories, each more plausible than the last. With every word, Peter felt his confidence surge, a tide rising within him, bolstered by the steady stream of potential leads. Thompson's words painted vivid pictures of scenarios. Peter's notes became a roadmap to navigating the treacherous terrain of the case.

'Could Phyllis's gossip-mill have churned out any kernels of truth amidst the chaff?' Thompson mused, stroking his chin. 'Or is Lister our man?

'You have a point about Phyllis. She might spin tales taller than the church spire, but there's often a thread of truth tangled up in her yarns,' Peter chuckled, etching her name beside a question mark. 'As for Lister, he's in gaol.'

'Have you checked?'

Thompson's question struck Peter like a bolt of lightning. How could he have forgotten to check the obvious? He knew his mistake in basic policing might cost Ant and Lyn their lives.

'Ah, you haven't. I see,' said Thompson with a heavy sigh. 'No matter. A call to the prison will settle that question. I'll leave you to do that, eh?'

'I'm sorry, Sam. I failed to cover the basics.'

'Stop it, Peter. Feeling sorry for yourself doesn't suit you. You're too close to this one, that's all. We've all done it... Yes, even me. The trick is to fix it, not beat yourself up. Doing that doesn't do anyone any good, especially the two people you're trying to protect. Got it?' Thompson offered Peter a fatherly smile.

'Got it,' replied the detective, meeting his mentor's supportive look square on.

'That's the ticket, Peter.'

'Thank you, Sam. I won't let them down,' Peter said with a determination that surprised even himself.

'Nor will you let yourself down,' Thompson replied, his

tone softening. 'Now, off you go. There's a mystery out there with your name on it, just waiting to be solved.'

'Yes, Guv,' Peter said, rising to his feet with a renewed sense of purpose.

Thompson let out a roar. 'Goodness, it's been a long time since anyone called me that. To tell you the truth, I rather miss it all. Anyway, onwards and all that.'

'And I miss working for you,' Peter responded.

'Do you remember the "Great Biscuit Heist of '96?"' Thompson began. The glow from the desk light cast an animated glow on his face, one lined with the wisdom of years and the subtle mirth of reminiscences. 'It seemed trivial, biscuits going missing from the local cafe. But it was the pattern, the meticulousness that unravelled the case.'

Peter watched, captivated, as his mentor's hands danced through the air, mimicking the stealthy swipe of the biscuit pilferer. 'You always said to look for the pattern,' Peter replied, his admiration for Thompson's expertise clear.

'Indeed,' Thompson confirmed with a nod. 'Patterns, Peter. Patterns are the whispers of intent amidst the clamour of coincidence.'

'Like the invitation,' Peter mused. 'Too deliberate to be a random threat.'

'Exactly!' Thompson exclaimed, slapping his knee. 'You're sharpening up, lad. Now, Thompson leaned forward, elbows on his desk piled high with books, and said, 'Sometimes, you find the solution where you least expect it. Think about who benefits from such theatrics? Who wants the wedding derailed?'

Peter mulled over Thompson's words, his thoughts threading together disparate pieces of information like a master weaver at a loom. His pen scratched across the paper as if it were pulling the very essence of clarity from the inkwell of advice before him.

'Sometimes,' Thompson continued, easing forward, elbows resting on the mountains of books that guarded his desk. 'You find the solution in the place you least expect.

'It all leads back to Lister, doesn't it?'

A gust of wind howled against the study window, as if laughing at the imagery, and Peter chuckled.

'Some things never change. That man is still causing trouble.'

'Always the minor details, Peter. They'll lead you home.'

'I won't forget your help, Sam,' Peter said as he neared the front door. 'I know what my next move is now.'

'Good man,' Thompson replied with a warm smile. 'And remember, every mystery solved begins with the courage to ask the right questions, or in your case, telephone call.'

With those parting words, Peter stepped outside, his frame straightening with newfound resolve. His notebook was now bulging with scribbles and underlines, each a beacon toward the truth.

As Peter neared his police car, Thompson called out.

'Luck is simply opportunity meeting preparation. You're prepared. Now seize the opportunity!'

The house door shut, leaving Thompson in the warm embrace of his study. Outside, Peter started the engine as his mind raced with possibilities. The afternoon sun mirrored Peter's anticipation of discovery. He pondered Sam's wisdom as he disappeared into rural Norfolk's network of narrow roads. One thing he knew; he had to make that telephone call.

Thursday, 4th September: 4.40 pm

PETER RILEY CLIMBED the familiar steps of Stanton Parva police station and strode into the small reception area with purpose. 'Anything interesting?' he asked the desk sergeant.

'Nothing of interest, Sir,' came the reply.

'I'll be in my office if anyone needs me...but if it's rubbish, tell them I'm not in, will you?'

'Will do. Mug of tea and a Kit Kat, is it?'

'You're a marvel, Sergeant. Bring it on.'

Once safely seated in his office, his mind replayed his mentor's counsel, each word a stepping stone across the murky waters of the case that had consumed him. An image of Ant and Lyn flickered in the forefront of his consciousness. 'I've got to sort this for them,' he murmured.

He reached into his pocket, feeling the crisp edges of the notes he'd taken during his meeting with Thompson. With each step, he planned strategies in his mind like the grand reveal at a village fete. He'd start by ringing the prison that held Lister. Next, he'd dissect his past, peeling back layers of deception as one would skin an overripe apple from the community orchard.

'Ah, Lister,' he imagined, 'what are you up to?'

The church clock chimed, its sonorous tones marking the passing of time. Fear was a luxury Peter could not afford, and so he traded it for focus, the kind that sharpened his senses and made the afternoon seem alive with hidden clues.

'Thompson said to look beyond the obvious,' Peter recalled. He thought of the retired detective's advice to consider every angle, every unlikely scenario. 'Well then, let's dance with the improbable.'

A smirk played upon his lips as he imagined confronting

Lister, watching the shock ripple across the man's face when he realised none other than his onetime subordinate had thwarted that his carefully crafted plot.

Peter opened his desk drawer and consulted a lengthy list of telephone number. His finger rested on one in particular, His Majesty's Prison, Duffield.

Picking up his mobile, he carefully pressed the keypad. It felt like he'd waited an age for someone to answer. Then his waiting was over.

'Afternoon. This is Detective Inspector Peter Riley of the Norfolk Constabulary. May I speak to the governor on an urgent police matter, please?'

After what seemed like an age while they took him through the required security measures, a gruff voice answered. 'Detective Inspector Riley. What can I do for you?'

Peter knew the man. He had a well-earned reputation for not suffering fools lightly. He also knew he'd only have a few seconds to make his request clear, before the hardened prison boss simply put the 'phone down on him.

'Afternoon, Governor. Can you tell me if Lister remains at your facility?' Peter knew he sound harsh, but knew the governor expected him to be short.

'Don't you people read your bulletins? ex-Commander Lister escaped six-weeks ago. Blast the man.'

Just at that moment, the sergeant entered with a mug of tea and a plate nestling two Kit Kats. 'Is anything the matter, Sir?' asked the concerned officer.

Peter's face had drained of colour as he looked at his mobile, unable to speak. He looked at the desk Sargeant without seeing until the voice bellowing out of his mobile's speaker shook him from his stupor.

'Yes, yes. I'm here.'

'Why are you ringing? Have you information to help us recapture the prisoner?'

Peter knew he couldn't avoid telling the man about his concerns.

'Keep me informed. When you get a confirmed sighting, ring me at once. At once, do you understand?'

The governor didn't wait for Peter's response, leaving the detective holding his mobile mid-air.

'Sir?'

Peter eventually acknowledged his officer.

'Er, yes. Thank you. Just put it down, will you?'

'Can I help at all, Sir? You look dreadful.'

Peter hesitated. Seconds passed before he pulled himself together. 'Does the name Lister ring a bell with you?'

'Him? Is it that bent ex chief inspector that's causing all this rumpus? I thought he was still in the clink?'

'So did I,' Peter said mournfully. 'He escaped, and now he's after revenge on Anthony Stanton and Lyn Blackthorn.'

The worry on each man's face mirrored the other.

'Not a word, Sergeant. Not until I brief the team. Understood?'

'Understood, Sir,' replied the desk sergeant as he left the office and closed the door behind him.

After ten minutes of reflection to allow the disturbing news to sink in, Peter determined he needed some fresh air. He knew his next decision could determine whether his close friends lived or faced a terrible fate.

'This time you really haven't seen me, OK?' Peter said as he strode through the reception and out of the police station.

'Yes—'

Peter didn't wait to hear the sergeant's full response.

He turned left and walked at speed until he's cleared the village and broke into open countryside. The flat landscape stretched out before Peter, the vast expanse of green calming his racing mind. His thoughts darted like a flock of starlings, never settling on one clear path. The sun dipped lower in the sky, casting long shadows that seemed to point in different directions, mimicking the confusion in his head.

As he walked, a cool breeze carried the aroma of a nearby apple orchard and distant smoke from a cottage. Peter's eyes scanned the horizon, searching for something, anything, that could give him a clue as to Lister's where-abouts. The responsibility pressed down on him, urging him to act decisively.

A sudden gust of wind tugged at his coat, as if nature itself was trying to push him in a certain direction. And then it hit him - the derelict remains of Hove House on the outskirts of Stanton Parva. Rumoured abounded that ghosts inhabit the ruin. A perfect hiding spot for someone like Lister. Peter couldn't help smiling at the irony of a spectre keeping the resident ghost company.

Peter quickened his pace, his shoes crunched on the gravel path beneath him as he made his way towards Hove House. The eerie silhouette of the old mansion loomed ahead, its windows boarded up and ivy creeping up the cracked walls. As he approached, a sense of foreboding washed over him.

The front door creaked ominously as he pushed it open, revealing a dimly lit interior shrouded in shadows. Cobwebs danced in the faint light filtering through gaps in the window boards, and the musty scent of neglect clinging to every surface.

'Mr. Lister?' Peter called out, his voice echoing through the abandoned halls. Silence greeted him in return, broken only by the occasional scuttle of a small creature seeking refuge in the decaying walls.

Drawing his flashlight, Peter ventured further into the house, his footsteps muffled by the thick layer of dust covering every surface. Room after room yielded nothing but space and echoes.

Satisfied that Lister wasn't there, he made his way back to what remained of the front entrance door. As he did so, he felt something underfoot. 'Probably detritus,' he murmured. He stepped back and stooped to inspect the item. A broad smile broke across his face. 'So, you have been here,' he said aloud, too excited to keep the news to himself.

The detective put a scene of crime glove on his right hand to retrieve the small object. A half-used stick of sealing wax gave off a dull reflection under the interrogation of his penlight.

'Never discount the wind, Peter,' Thompson had said, his voice rich in the timbre of experience. 'It can shift directions when you least expect it, much like the motives of a cunning adversary.'

'Thank you for guiding me, Sam,' Peter whispered.

As he strolled along Stanton Parva's uneven high street, he drank in the tradition enveloping the village, just as he, a modern detective, utilised ancient sleuthing skills. The detective's reflections ceased as his mobile rang. 'Riley,' he answered, his tone shifting from introspective to alert.

'Peter, it's Lyn. Something's happened,' came the trembling voice on the other end, edged with panic. 'There's been another note.'

His heart skipped a beat, and for a second, the world seemed to stop, even the wind holding its breath. This was a twist he hadn't expected.

'Stay put, I'm on my way,' he assured her before ending the call. As he broke into a jog, the stakes now higher than ever, Peter knew one thing for certain: the game was afoot, and there was no room for error. With Thompson's guidance echoing in his mind and Lister's hideout discovered, he readied himself for what lay ahead.

Chapter Five

OLD TED

Thursday, 4th September: 7.20 pm

THE OLD SCHOOLHOUSE had a calm and peaceful atmosphere on Thursday evening, with its ivy-clad walls adding a touch of history. Peter's shoes crunched on the gravel path as he hurried to Lyn's front door, his shadow elongating in the last rays of the sun. The rap of his knuckles against the wood was urgent.

Lyn greeted him at the threshold, her usually bright eyes clouded by recent events.

'Good to see you, Peter. He's sent another one. Well, not an invitation. A note. It's horrible.'

'Let's have a look, shall we?' Peter said in a calm voice, attempting to reassure her as they made their way into the kitchen.

With a slight tremor, she showed the chilling note that invaded her home - 'I'm getting closer - sweet poetry indeed.'

'Same handwriting as before,' Peter observed, his voice

steady despite the undercurrent of frustration. 'Lister takes perverse glee in these threats.'

'Sweet poetry?' Lyn scoffed lightly, not allowing fear to rob her of composure. 'More like the ramblings of a coward.'

Peter nodded, his brows knitting together. 'I know I've said it before, but this time I seriously think you should post-pone the wedding. This man is methodical, persistent. He's not going away.'

Lyn's jaw set with a determined resolve, her blue eyes flashing with defiance. She shook her head firmly. 'No, Peter. We won't let him dictate our lives. The wedding will go on as planned.'

Peter regarded her with admiration and worry, knowing the strength that lay within Lyn but also fearing for her safety. 'I understand your determination, but I've got to think about your safety now. We don't know where Lister is, or what he's up to, other than intent on doing you harm.'

The movement of the latch announced Ant's arrival before his tall frame filled the doorway, tension carved into his features. 'You too?' he asked, directing his gaze toward Lyn.

Her simple nod told him everything he needed to know. The shine in her eyes betraying the bravado of her stance. Ant crossed the kitchen in two strides, enveloping her in a reassuring embrace that spoke volumes of their shared resolve.

'Look at this,' Ant said, breaking the silence as he handed over his own ominous note to Peter. He read it aloud. 'How can a man who trained as an intelligence officer be so stupid? Poetic justice, perhaps?'

'It just adds insult to injury, doesn't it?' Peter muttered, folding the paper with precision. 'Anthony, I've advised Lyn already, but with you here now, we should seriously consider—'

'Postponing?' Ant interrupted, the word hanging between them like a spectre. They exchanged looks, each one laden with unspoken thoughts.

'Less than 48 hours' notice,' Lyn murmured, her tone wistful, yet edged with defiance. 'But if we delay, when will we ever be safe?'

'Exactly,' Ant agreed, his jaw setting in determination. 'If he doesn't make his move on our wedding day, he'll try another time. We can't let him dictate our lives.'

'If you're sure...?' Peter's question came softly.

'We are,' Ant replied.'

'In one sense, I agree with you both. He'll have expected you might call off the wedding. Lister will, I'm certain, have a backup plan; ready to strike when least expected.'

In rural Norfolk, amidst a tapestry of lush fields and age-old trees, the decision held. Whatever shadows lurked beyond the hedgerows, Lyn, and Ant would face them together. They knew Peter would do everything in his power to keep them safe, by his determination to bring the malicious poet to justice.

The evening's waning sun casts a golden glow across the Old Schoolhouse, painting the quaint brickwork with a warmth that belied the chill. Inside, the atmosphere was far from warm.

'I don't want to make matters worse than they already are,' Peter began.

'What do you mean?' Lyn answered, her features tensing.

Peter pulled an evidence bag from the depths of his jacket. His grim features matched the gravity of his news.

'Lister has escaped from prison, so we know for sure

now that he's behind all of this,' he announced, voice steady but eyes betraying his words. Lyn and Ant froze, their hands still clasped from moments before, now gripping each other as if bracing for a storm.

'Escaped?' Lyn's voice barely rising above a whisper, her mind racing through the implications. 'So, it's definitely ex Commander Lister we're looking for?'

'I'm afraid so.' Peter placed the evidence bag on the kitchen table, where the fading light caught on the red flecks of sealing wax within. 'I found this at a derelict house I stumbled across on the outskirts of the village.'

Lyn leaned in closer, her keen eyes comparing the wax to the envelope. 'It's the same,' she confirmed, her usually confident nature edged by a newfound intensity. 'He's been here all the time?'

'Which means maybe he's watching us right now,' Ant added, scanning the windows as if expecting shadows to move.

'Which is why I've arranged a stakeout at the derelict house,' Peter interjected quickly, meeting their alarmed looks with a reassuring nod. 'My officers will keep watch continuously until you're married and off on your honeymoon. If Lister so much as sneezes, we'll know.'

'Thank you, Peter,' Ant said, the tension in his shoulders easing slightly. 'At least there's some comfort in knowing we know where he's been, and we have police eyes out there.'

Peter cracked a rare smile, his gaze sweeping over Lyn's determined face and Ant's protective stance. 'We might not have the bardic flair of our uninvited guest, but when it's about protecting our own, we write a better story.'

The light-hearted quip didn't quite banish the worry etched in their expressions, but it reminded them of the togetherness they shared.

'Let's hope it's a snooze fest at that old house,' Lyn said, trying to inject some humour back into the room. 'For all our sakes.'

'I's possible in one sense, you may be right. The problem with that is, if he doesn't go back to the ruin. The three friends paused in silence, trying to understand the significance of Lister freely wandering in Stanton Parva. it'll beg the question of where he is.'

A moment of contemplative silence fell. The three friends absorbed the implications of Lister roaming in and around Stanton Parva, unmolested. Leaving the twisted jail-breaker to do his worst.

'I doubt Lister is one to rest on his laurels,' Peter said.

'Then neither shall we,' Ant declared, squeezing Lyn's hand tighter. The trio paused in silence, processing the fact that Lister was freely wandering around Stanton Parva.

'Lister knows this area too well,' Peter observed, his brows knitting together. 'He's navigating with a precision that suggests inside help.'

Ant nodded, rubbing his chin thoughtfully. 'Remember when Lister was here for the Amber Burton case? The one he ordered you to stand down from. He was like a fox in the henhouse, slipping in and out before anyone knew what hit them.'

Lyn's eyes narrow, the gears in her head turning. 'Do you think someone from back then could assist him?'

Peter's expression darkened as he considered Lyn's question. 'It's a possibility we can't ignore,' he admitted. 'During his time in Stanton Parva, Lister could have easily made connections with individuals willing to bend the rules for their own gain.'

Ant's jaw clenched at the thought of a traitor within

their community aiding their enemy. 'We must discover who might collude with him,' he stated, his voice firm.

Lyn's mind raced. 'The thing is, we know who crossed paths with Lister during his previous visit.' Her eyes widened as a realisation struck her. 'If that's the case, then it's someone we know who's helping him. How could that be? It's too awful to think about.'

The trio exchanged worried glances as they thought through the consequences.

'Let's not jump too quickly. We know intimidation is second nature to that awful creature,' Ant commented, his voice low but steady. 'But either way, it maybe that we're dealing with more than just one man's vendetta.'

'Which is why we need to redouble our efforts to find him,' Peter stated decisively. 'We'll blanket the village and the surrounding area, have eyes on every corner.'

'We shouldn't overlook the less obvious routes,' Lyn interjected. 'He may have come by bus or train. No car sightings, right?'

'True,' Peter admitted, his hand absently brushing his chin. 'That makes things trickier if he's moving around on foot or public transport.'

'Then we'll just have to be even more vigilant,' Lyn said with a determined tilt to her jaw. 'We can't let this... this poet of peril shape our lives.'

'Poet of peril,' Ant chuckled. 'I like it. Let us welcome the bard of Stoney Stanton!'

'Every village needs one,' Lyn quipped, a playful glint in her eye.

The trio continued to exchange banter to maintain normality in a situation that was the opposite.

'Right,' Peter says, rubbing his hands together, 'Enough of the joking. I have a plan. My officers can only do so much, given how thin on the ground they are. I'll try the local constabularies, but I don't hold much hope out for being able to borrow any officers. That leaves one solution. We need village volunteers to fill the gaps. Any ideas?'

Ant and Lyn thought for a short time. 'Let's ask Fitch and Sophie. They won't mind helping,' suggested Lyn, her voice steady despite her inner worries. 'They have a knack for noticing... oddities. I'll also ring my school secretary. Tina's always up for an adventure.'

Ant nodded, picturing the alert pair who ran the local garage. 'I'll ring some of my estate workers. They're used to keeping watch over the grounds.' He pauses, a smile tugging at his lips. 'And I know my parents would love to help, but they aren't exactly spring chickens anymore.'

Lyn chuckled, the sound light. 'Well, it's certainly no use asking my parents. They'd be too busy bickering to spot a fly, let alone Lister. After all these years of being divorced, and living in the same village, you'd think they'd learn to get along, but no. They still argue like stubborn teenagers.'

'Let's hope our other villagers are more observant,' Peter quips, his eyes twinkling with mirth. 'OK, let's get going. I'll nip to the station and get my lot sorted. I'll leave you to ring your contacts. Let's meet up in the village hall in one hour. I know it's getting late, but I'm sure any volunteers you muster won't mind.'

The time soon slipped by. The village had a buzz to it with eager volunteers waiting for Peter's briefing. Uniformed officers mixed with locals, each person eager to get going.

Phyllis, the village's self-appointed news anchor, had caught wind of the proceedings. Betty, her steadfast shadow, stood by her side.

'Inspector Riley,' Phyllis called out, cutting through the

chatter like a knife through butter. 'I insist on being part of this operation. It's our duty to protect Lord Anthony and his bride to be.'

Peter approached. 'Phyllis, your talents lie not out there in the cold. You have a gift for... gathering information.'

'Indeed, I do,' she replied, looking about the room to ensure all heard the detective's compliment.

'Then it's settled,' Peter announced grandly. 'You shall commandeer my office at the station. Make it your head-quarters. Coordinate the comings and goings, relay messages. We need someone with your... unique skills to keep us informed.'

Phyllis preened herself under the praise, clearly delighted with her promotion. Betty, meanwhile, gave Peter a knowing look and smile to match, both unseen by her companion. 'Well, if you insist,' Phyllis said.

'Off you go then,' Peter encouraged, ushering both ladies toward the door. 'And remember, no detail is too small.'

With Phyllis and Betty dispatched, Peter stood on the small stage. His eyes scanned the assembled volunteers—a motley crew of villagers and constables, each one poised to play their part in the unfolding drama. He cleared his throat; a silence fell like a soft blanket over the room.

'Alright, listen up,' he began, voice steady as oak. 'We're looking for a disgraced senior police officer by the name of Lister. Many, if not all, of you will be familiar with that person. He's the one who...' His gaze drifted momentarily, acknowledging the shared memory of Amber Burton's untimely fate. Murmurs of assent rippled through the crowd; the air crackled with barely suppressed outrage.

'However,' Peter continued, raising a hand to command calm, 'Your mission is to observe and report only. If you spot him, do not engage. Use your mobile to report the matter. Make sure you keep a safe distance.'

He pierced them with a look that brooked no argument. 'Anger is our enemy tonight. It clouds judgement. We need cool heads. The last thing we want is to chase him off and for my officers to be back to square one.'

Nods around the room told him his message had hit home. With a last nod, the gathering dispersed for each to take up their allotted position.

Back at the police station, Peter slumped against the tall counter in reception. His earlier adrenaline was now replaced by a niggling regret. He reflected that offering his office to Phyllis might be the mistake of the century. A sigh emanated as he caught the eye of the desk sergeant. Even his usual stoicism had worn thin because of the relentless barrage of tea requests and biscuit enquiries from the office's occupants.

'Garibaldi biscuits, Peter,' the sergeant grumbled. 'She specifically asked for Garibaldi biscuits. I had to dig into my emergency stash.'

'Emergency stash?' Peter chuckled, then winced as another demand came from within the office turned 'head-quarters.'

The ring of his mobile cut through the impending doom. Peter answered swiftly, heart racing. A villager claimed to have seen Lister entering an abandoned signal box on the old railway line that skirted Stanton Parva. The detective consulted the map sprawled on the counter; fingers traced the line to the location given. Just as he was about to dash for his car, the mobile rang out again. Peter's disappointment was. 'A false alarm, you say.' Peter listened intently to the caller. 'Who is Old Ted?' he asked. 'Oh, I see. Well, thank you for letting me know.' Peter ended the call and slowly put his mobile back into a pocket.

'Now there's a character,' said the desk sergeant. 'He comes through here two or three times a year; has done for decades. He means no harm, but he doesn't half pong...and do not get me started on his clothes. They must grow on him.'

Peter considered matters. But the villager said he wore new clothes, that's why he thought it was our man?'

'Old Ted,' chuckled the desk sergeant. 'More like he nicked them off a washing line.'

The mention of new garments sparked an idea, a thread to be pulled in this tangled web.

'I'm off to have a chat with our tailored gentleman of the road,' he announced. Already halfway to the door, the desk sergeant's goodbye became interrupted. Betty's hatted head poked out of Riley's office.

'Phyllis would like—'

'More Garibaldi biscuits,' replied the mournful sergeant. 'Coming up, Betty.'

Meanwhile, Peter's car crunched along the gravel path to the disused signal box, its headlights cutting through the night. He parked with a final skid of pebbles and stepped out into the cool Norfolk air, the earthy scent of damp foliage mingling with the mustiness of disrepair.

Old Ted sat perched on an upturned box, his new attire oddly crisp against the backdrop of rusted metal and peeling paint. His wary gaze followed Peter as he approached, a lifetime of mistrust etched in the lines around his eyes.

'Got a smoke?' Old Ted asked, hopeful yet sceptical.

'Sorry, I don't smoke,' Peter replied, his even tone betraying none of the urgency that griped him.

'Drink then? A bit o' the good stuff?'

'Sorry, never touch it. But how about ten pounds for a chat?' Peter suggested, pulling out the banknote like a magician revealing his last illusion.

Ted's attention snapped to the money, his eyes lit with glee and caution. He reached out, fingers almost brushing the crisp currency, but Peter was quicker, pulling it just out of reach.

'Let's talk about your clothes first. Where'd you find them?' Peter said in a non-threatening, but insistent manner.

'From a derelict house, didn't I?' Ted's hand waved dismissively toward an indeterminate point.

'Which house?' Peter insisted, still dangling the tenner like a carrot before a stubborn donkey.

'Over there, on the other side of the village. Up a gravel path,' Ted explained, his focus unwavering from the prize on offer. Another tug at the note, another failed attempt.

'Anyone there when you found them?' Peter inquired, finally allowing the note to slip into Ted's eager grasp.

'Didn't see no one. Clothes were in a pile, that's all.' Ted shrugged, already eyeing the exit now that he'd got his payment.

'Did you find anything in the pockets?' Peter asked, knowing full well the sort of treasures that can hide in discarded garments.

'Nothing. Tight git, whoever he was,' Ted scowled, but Peter was already moving in, patting down the coat with professional detachment.

'Let's make sure, shall we?' Peter announced, more to himself than Ted, who stood there, an immovable object of grime and newfound wealth.

And then, the feel of card against Peter's fingers. He pulled out a rail ticket, the evidence he didn't know he was seeking. 'At least we know where he left from and when he arrived,' Peter muttered.

'Train? Not me, mate. Haven't been on one since 1969. The British Rail sarnies were 'oriole. Never went on one again,' Ted replied with another scowl.

Peter ignored Ted's comment. His mind raced with the implications of the new clue. Were the pieces of the puzzle finally beginning to slot together? he thought. The answer lay close, hidden amidst the quaint charm of the village, and the secret trails trod by wildlife. With the ticket tucked securely in his pocket, Peter nodded at Ted, his next move already forming in the maze of his thoughts.

Chapter Six

TICKET TO RIDE

Friday, 5th September: 9.30 am

THE SUN DRAPED its first golden rays across the dewy fields of Norfolk, a herald to the tranquil morning. At Lil's Tuck Wagon, nestled among the whispering reeds and the occasional sleepy bleat of distant sheep, Ant, Lyn and Peter have converged like adventurers of old around a wobbly metal table that had seen better days.

'Right,' Lyn began, brushing back a wayward strand of her shoulder-length blond hair, the early light giving it an almost ethereal glow. 'We can't just sit here sipping tea and eating bacon sandwiches. What do we do next?'

Ant rubbed his chin thoughtfully, the creases in his forehead deepened with concern. 'I don't know. What about Stanton's newsagent? Lister clearly fancies himself as a poet. There might be a trail of ink leading back to him.'

Peter nodded, his right hand firmly gripping his bacon sandwich for breakfast. 'Plus, Mr. Mellor sees everyone. If Lister's been around, he'd know.'

'It's got to be worth a go,' Lyn replied, determination lighting up her green eyes. She took a sip from her chipped mug and set it down on the wobbly metal table-top with a clink. After another ten minutes of finishing their snack, the trio took their empty mugs and cleared plates to the tuck wagon.

'See you all again soon,' chirped Lil, a woman who always had a cheery smile for her customers.

'Can't wait,' Lyn said, as the three friends each climbed into their respective cars and drove in convoy back to Stanton Parva.

They strolled through the village, past cottages with roses clinging to their stone walls, greeting early risers with a polite nod or a cheery 'morning'.

As they entered the newsagent, the smell of newsprint and confectionery enveloped them, with rows of magazines and sweets standing sentinel along the walls.

'Morning, Mr. Mellor,' Lyn said as she greeted the proprietor, a portly man with spectacles sliding down his nose.

'Morning, all!' Mr. Mellor replied with a warm smile, abandoning his task of stacking newspapers. 'What brings you three in so early? Not running out of stamps, are you?'

'Actually, we're wondering if you've noticed any unfamiliar faces around lately,' Ant said, leaning against the counter. 'Particularly anyone who might've bought a calligraphy pen or the like?'

'New faces, eh?' Mr. Mellor stroked his chin, pondering the question. 'Well, now that you mention it, there was this one chap—a friendly sort. Looked like he hadn't been in a newsagent for years, marvelled at everything. He bought an old calligraphy set gathering dust in the window. Said something about needing it for a special occasion.'

'Did he now?' Peter interjected, exchanging a quick glance with Ant. 'And did this man leave a name or anything else that could tell us more about him?'

'Name? No, no, but he had a familiar air about him,' Mr. Mellor replied, shrugging apologetically. 'Sorry, I can't be of more help. But if he comes back for another chat, I will let you know.'

'Thanks, Mr. Mellor,' Lyn said with a grateful smile. 'You've been more help than you realise.'

The three exchanged hopeful looks as they stepped back outside under the widening sky, their spirits buoyed by the prospect of a new lead.

'Off to a good start,' Ant remarked, his gaze following a pheasant as it strutted regally across the road. 'Let's keep the momentum going. Now we need to find a wedding stationer nearby that might have sold our man the invitations he sent.'

'Problem is, he may have brought them with him,' Lyn said.

'May be, he did,' added Peter. 'But it's got to be worth a punt. I say we have a go.'

———

Friday, 5th September: 1.10 pm

THE BELL above the door announced their arrival as Ant, Lyn, and Peter shuffled into Duval's Wedding Stationers in Runcton Longville, the nearest such vendor to Stanton Parva. The smell of paper and ink mingled with a faint aroma of beeswax. Rows of colourful invitations and elegant gift bags spoke of hopeful futures and joyful unions.

'Can I help you?' Mrs. Hennigan, the shop owner, asked

as she emerged from behind a display of embossed envelopes.

'I hope so,' Lyn said, producing the photograph they had been carrying around like a talisman. 'Do you recognise this man?'

Mrs. Hennigan squinted at the image, shook her head, then reached for a pair of thick-rimmed glasses. Once perched firmly on her face, the woman's expression shifted. 'Hang on, put glasses on that man and—yes, yes, I remember him!' she exclaimed, tapping the photo with a fingertip. 'Came in here a few days ago, browsed through our wedding invitations. Took his sweet time about it too.'

Ant leaned in; his interest piqued. 'Did he say what he was looking for? You know, anything specific?'

'Only that he was organising a big wedding,' Mrs Hennigan recalled, frowning as she tries to summon up the details from memory. 'I had to hurry him along in the end; my stomach doesn't tolerate late lunches.'

'Did he purchase anything?' Lyn inquired, her detective instincts sharpening.

'Ah, no, he didn't.' Mrs. Hennigan replied, 'But—I gave him two samples to choose from. He seemed taken with them.'

'Can you recall which ones were they?' Peter asked, anticipation threading through his voice.

'Oh yes. They're our most popular. Let me show you.' Mrs Hennigan bustled off, returning moments later with two samples in hand.

'They're identical to the design that had arrived unso-licited at Ant and Lyn's doorstep,' Peter declared.

'Curious,' Ant muttered, regarding the samples as if they might spring to life and confess their secrets.

'Thank you, Mrs Hennigan. You've been most helpful,' Ant said.

'Always glad to assist,' the shopkeeper replied with a grandiose wave, as if a member of the Royal Family on the balcony of Buckingham Palace.

Outside, the trio paused, letting the morning sun warm their faces as they considered their next move, as a tractor ambled past, trailing a cloud of dust and the faint smell of freshly mown grass.

Lyn cast a quick glance at her wristwatch. 'I've got to dash for my final fitting,' she announced, her voice laced with both excitement and stress.

'Take the Morgan,' Ant suggested, tossing her the keys with a reluctant smile. 'Just try not to treat the gearbox like it's an unruly pupil needing discipline.'

'Hilarious,' Lyn retorted with a warmth in her laughter as she caught the keys like an expert cricketer.

'Remember, it's all about finesse,' Peter called after her, earning himself a playful scowl over Lyn's shoulder.

'Since when did you become such a motoring expert?' she quipped before slipping into the driver's seat, the leather creaking a welcome beneath her.

The engine roared to life, a throaty promise of power. Ant winced as Lyn engaged first gear with more enthusiasm than skill. The sound of grinding metal echoed briefly before the car lurched forward and sped off at a rate of knots.

'She'll get the hang of it,' Peter chuckled, watching the car disappear down the village road, a plume of dust kicking up behind it.

'Let's hope my car survives until the honeymoon,' Ant mused, half-joking, half-genuine in his concern for his beloved vintage sports car.

'Come on.' Peter clapped him on the back and steered him away from the receding cloud of dust. 'We've got a snake to catch, not to mention a wedding to protect.'

'Right,' Ant agreed, folding himself into the police car. Within seconds, Peter set his course to take the car to the police station.

The station was a hive of muted activity, officers moving with purpose amidst the buzz of radios and ringing 'phones. Ant and Peter approached the front desk, where the sergeant greeted them with a nod of recognition.

'Afternoon. Back on the Lister trail, I assume?'

'Indeed,' Peter replied. 'We need to dig into his past—addresses, known associates, that sort of stuff. And we're wondering if his son might still be in Lister's orbit.'

'Ah, the apple doesn't fall far from the tree, does it?' the sergeant mused. 'I'll fetch the files for you. Then tea?'

A few minutes later, and the sergeant opened the door to Peter's office.

'Here we are,' the sergeant remarked, holding a thick folder stamped with 'Lister, Ian', in bold letters. 'Everything we've got on him.'

'Thanks,' Peter replied, taking the file. For the next few minutes, he leafed through the papers, leaving Ant to ponder what might emerge. The detective's eyes scanned quickly for any clue that might lead them closer to thwarting the plotter's sinister plan. Ant leaned in beside him, equally intent on finding that one thread that could unravel the entire scheme.

'Seems like a family affair,' Peter murmured, tapping a photo of Lister's son. 'Wonder if he's helping his father?'

'Wouldn't put it past them,' Ant agrees, his brow furrowed in concentration. 'But let's not jump to conclusions just yet.'

'Fair point,' Peter conceded. 'We'll follow the evidence wherever it leads.'

'That's what you always tell Lyn and me,' Ant replied, closing the file with a snap. 'And right now, it's leading us to some old-fashioned detective work.'

'Sounds like a plan,' Peter replied.

Then came a sharp rap on the office door as the desk sergeant entered with two mugs of tea.

'Phyllis's been through here like a hurricane again,' the sergeant grumbled, pushing his glasses up the bridge of his nose. 'Cleaned us out of biscuits, she did.'

Peter shook his head, half amused, and shrugged nonchalantly. 'It'll just have to be tea, then.'

'Speaking of hurricanes,' Ant began. 'This wedding is shaping up to be quite the spectacle.'

'Your aristocratic lot mingling with the village folk?' Peter chuckled. 'I can see it now: top hats and tweed amidst the bunting and beer tents.'

'Count on Lyn's mum putting on airs, trying to outdo everyone,' Ant said, his eyes sparkling with mischief. 'And my father attempting to smooth things over with stories of his military escapades.'

'Bound to be memorable,' Peter agreed with a grin. 'Just hope your best man's speech is ready. Wouldn't want Fitch fumbling over his words.'

'Ah, the speech,' Ant mused aloud, momentarily distracted by the thought. 'He'll have it off to a tee, and I'm dreading what tales about me he's going to slip in.'

Stepping out into the sunlit street a little later, the sight of Fitch wrestling with a Cornish Pasty greeted the pair, its flaky crust crumbling at the edges. As he noticed them, he chomped down enthusiastically, only to spray crumbs in a wide arc as he attempted to speak.

'Watch it, Fitch!' Ant exclaimed, stepping back with a laugh. 'You're worse than the pigeons in Trafalgar Square!'

'Sorry, lads,' Fitch coughed through his pastry-stuffed mouth. 'How's the hunt for the elusive Mr. Lister? Not... too distracting, I hope, with your last day of bachelorhood upon us.'

'Hmm, yes, the round of drinks at the Wherry Arms,' Ant recalled, the memory bringing a slight grimace to his face. 'A moment of generosity I might live to regret.'

'Generosity or the ale talking?' Peter teased, landing a hand on Ant's shoulder. 'Either way, we'll make sure you don't escape this evening without lightening that wallet of yours.'

'Cheers for that,' Ant replied, the good-natured ribbing a welcome respite from the tension of their investigation.

'Where are you two of to, then?' Fitch asked.

'Norwich Train Station. We want to check if they have any images of our man.'

'Sounds a lot more fun than having your head stuck in the clapped-out engine of an old Bedford lorry, 'cos that's what I'll be doing for the next three hours,' Fitch complained.

'No wonder your Sophie calls you her little oily rag,' Ant replied with a friendly smile.

With a last wave to Fitch, they set off, leaving behind the aroma of baked goods and the sound of villager dancing to the steps of its daily routine.

The police car's engine hummed steadily as Peter navigated the narrow country lanes, flanked by hedgerows bursting with the summer's late growth. Ant gazed out of the passenger window, watching as fields of green and gold rolled by and combine harvesters brought in the crop. The tranquillity of Norfolk's countryside contrasted with the tension that gripped him.

'Norwich station could be our best shot at catching the latest likeness of Lister,' Ant mused, breaking the comfortable silence. 'I mean, he wouldn't dare travel as himself, not with every copper in the county on the lookout for him.'

'True,' Peter agreed, his eyes fixed on the road. 'But if he's clever enough to escape from prison, he'll know we'd be checking the stations.' A wry smile played on his lips. 'Let's just hope his vanity got the better of him and he couldn't resist the chase.'

Ant chuckled, imagining the self-important fugitive primping before an unseen camera. 'Fancy glasses and casual clothes won't fool us. Lister's the type who irons his socks.'

'Speaking of fancy, how are you holding up with the wedding prep?' Peter asked, glancing with a teasing grin. 'Ready to face the firing squad of aristocrats and village folk?'

'Ha! It's like preparing for a re-enactment of the Kett's rebellion,' Ant replied with good humour. 'Lyn's parents alone are enough to send a man running for the hills. But I wouldn't miss it for the world.'

Their banter continued until they reached the outskirts of Norwich, the cityscape gradually overtaking the pastoral views. Soon, the police car pulled off Thorpe Road and into the station's car park.

Peter presented his credentials to the security supervisor, a stern-faced woman with a no-nonsense ponytail and short fringe. She nodded curtly and lead them through the maze of corridors to her office.

'Here we are,' she announced, pulling up the video file

on her computer with a few clicks. 'This is from the date and time you specified.'

Ant leaned forward; his eyes sharp as he scrutinised the footage. Grainy figures come and go, a ballet of commuters and luggage. The pair watched intently, rewinding, and pausing the video when a man resembling Lister appeared.

'Is that...?' Peter begins, pointing at the screen.

'Could be,' Ant replied, squinting at the small screen. 'Except Lister wouldn't be caught dead in a hoodie.'

'Wait, there!' Peter exclaimed as another figure crossed the frame. This time the man was taller, his gait familiar even in the pixelated images. And there he was—glasses perched on his nose, a casual jacket replacing the expected suit.

'Blimey, he's done it,' Ant whispered, a mixture of admiration and frustration colouring his voice. 'Ian 'Suit-and-Tie' Lister, going incognito in leisurewear and backpack. Look at the size of that case he's pulling behind him. Clever. Just like any other tourist.'

'Never thought I'd see the day,' Peter added, shaking his head with a chuckle. Now let's see if we can gather evidence from where his ticket said he got off the train.

With their lead confirmed, they thanked the still unsmiling security supervisor. Ant and Peter strode out of her office, already planning their next move in the dance of cat and mouse that winds through the fabric of Norfolk.

Friday, 5th September: 3.30 pm

GUNTON PARK STATION nestled like a well-kept secret amid the lush greenery of Norfolk's countryside. The building had an impeccably painted sign hanging from wrought iron brackets and flower baskets brimming with colour. Ant leaned out of the police car to admire the neatly trimmed hedges as Peter parked the unassuming police vehicle alongside a row of bicycles.

'Blimey, it's like stepping back a century,' Ant observed, his eyes tracing the ornate brickwork.

'Except for the lack of steam engines and top hats,' Peter quipped, closing the car door behind him with a soft click.

After a minute or two's search, the pair discovered the stationmaster, a ruddy-cheeked man with a smile that crinkled his eyes. As he swept the already spotless platform, Ant asked about CCTV coverage. The question elicited a hearty chuckle as the cheery stationmaster shook his head.

'This isn't London, you know,' the official remarked, leaning on his broom.

'Shame, they could have done with a measure of modern snooping tech,' Peter said, his lips curling upwards despite the frustration. He turned to Ant, confirming the expected absence of surveillance footage.

'Then it's down to good old-fashioned legwork,' Ant responded, rolling up his sleeves metaphorically.

Peter outlined the man in their sights to the stationmaster. The man listened intently before his expression brightened with recognition.

'Ah yes, the chap with the lively banter!' he exclaimed. 'Asked me about caravan parks, he did.'

'Caravan parks?' Peter repeated, surprised at his oversight.

'Silver Sands and Oak View,' the station-master supplies helpfully. 'They are the two nearest to us.'

'Thank you, much appreciated,' Peter said, tipping an imaginary cap as they parted ways.

Back in the car, Peter slammed the door harder than necessary. 'Camping grounds, Ant! How could I miss that?'

'Easy enough to do when you're chasing shadows,' Ant reassured him. They pulled away from the station, gravel crunching under tyres.

The first caravan site, Silver Sands, sprawled out like a small town, with row upon row of static mobile homes glittering under the morning sun. Peter's frown deepened as he took in the task's size ahead.

'Bit bigger than I expected,' he muttered, scratching his chin.

'Divide and conquer?' Ant suggested with a raised eyebrow.

'Right,' Peter agrees, looking determined. 'You stay here and do this one while I drive over to Oak View. Pick you up here in ninety minutes?'

'See you then,' Ant nods, watching Peter drive off before heading into the maze of caravans.

———

Friday, 5th September: 4.30 pm

PETER'S POLICE car pulled up with a soft crunch on the gravel path, the engine spluttering to a halt. He leaned over and pushed the passenger door open for Ant, who emerged from the depths of Silver Sands, looking every bit as fruitless in his search as Peter.

'Anything?' Peter asked, though the resignation in his eyes suggested he already knew the answer.

'Zilch,' Ant replied, dusting off his trousers which had gained a new shade of caravan-park-dust. 'You?'

'Same,' Peter sighs, drumming his fingers on the steering

wheel. 'I'm thinking Lister's sent us on another wild goose chase.'

'Left a trail of breadcrumbs for us, only they lead to nowhere,' Ant mused, climbing into the police car. They shared a glance, both considering the possibility that each clue was a deliberate misdirection.

'Could've seen Tom nosing around and dropped those clothes and ticket. You know, to set us scurrying in the wrong direction,' Peter suggested, reversing the car with a practised ease.

'Classic Lister, isn't it? The longer we chase our tails, the more time he has to plot,' Ant agreed.

'Exactly,' Peter said as he navigated Norfolk's rural hinterland, as he took his companion back to Stanton Hall.

———

Friday, 5th September: 5.15 pm

THE CLOCK TICKED AWAY in Peter's office as he slumped into his chair. He flipped through Lister's file once more, the same pages he'd been scouring earlier in the day, hoping for a hidden detail to jump out at him.

'Come on, you crafty old fox,' he muttered, scanning documents filled with Lister's known haunts, associates, and habits. The room was quiet except for the occasional flip of paper and the distant hubbub outside his window.

Then, like a lighthouse beam cutting through fog, a memory surfaced: Lister's son once mentioned his father's fondness for sailing. Peter's head snapped up, his eyes suddenly alight with the spark of an idea.

'Boats...' he whispered, reaching for a map of the

Norfolk Broads. His fingers traced the blue lines snaking their way through the countryside.

'Stanton Broad passes nearby the village, and Stanton Hall.' He leaned back in his chair, piecing together the potential movements of his quarry. 'He could hide in plain sight, playing captain of his own getaway vessel,' he mused aloud, the cogs turning rapidly now.

Grabbing his phone, he began jotting down the names and numbers of nearby boat hire companies. Duty called, and this duty might just involve a chase across the serene waters of the Norfolk Broads.

Peter's fingers danced across the keyboard with a haste that belayed his usual calm demeanour. Each tap echoed like a heartbeat racing against time. On his cluttered desk, amidst the scatter of police reports, lay a map speckled with red dots, each one marking the location of a boat hire company.

'Come on,' he muttered, as he zoomed into the digital map on his computer screen. He dragged the cursor over the winding waterways that crisscrossed the Norfolk landscape. Each represented a perfect hiding place for a man like Lister, who had the cunning to exploit such rustic serenity for nefarious ends.

'Stanton Broad, you sly devil,' Peter said, feeling frustrated with Lister's potential masterstroke. A simple leisure boat could be the last jigsaw piece in an otherwise perplexing puzzle. With each new entry added to his list, the enormity of the task ahead became more daunting. He knew there were too many possibilities for comfort, and time was slipping through his fingers like the fine grains of sand at Hunstanton beach.

'Who knew there were so many blasted boats in Norfolk?' he exclaimed, slapping a hand against his forehead. His eyes darted from the clock to the phone and back again. Peter knew full well that each passing moment brought Lister closer to executing his dark plan.

'Right, let's triage this,' he declared, his mind shifting gears from frantic to methodically strategic. He plotted a course, envisioning a systematic approach to canvass each hire company—a nautical needle in a haystack operation.

'Should've joined the coastguard instead of the force,' he quipped to himself, scribbling notes on a pad. In a race against time, Peter couldn't help grinning at the absurdity of chasing a fugitive through a maze of watery holiday retreats.

'Chasing shadows on the water...' he mused, hoping beyond hope his hunch might pay off. With a deep breath, he picked up the telephone receiver, ready to dial the first number on his list. This must work, he thought to himself.

Chapter Seven

THE LODGER

Friday, 5th September: 7.30 pm

DETECTIVE INSPECTOR PETER RILEY grew increasingly worried as he looked through his notes in his office. The looming threat of Ian Lister's vendetta had overshadowed the joyous bustle of the forthcoming nuptials. The former commander, once respected and admired, had become a bitter and mysterious figure. Worse still, he used his investigative skills for malicious purposes.

'Anything?' Fitch asked, leaning against the doorframe, his oil-stained overall rumpled from the day's work in his vehicle repair shop. Fitch's posture appeared relaxed, but concern in his eyes as he watched Peter thumb through his notes gave away his true thoughts.

'Boat hire companies all shut tight as a drum. Not a soul answering after hours,' Peter replied, massaging his temples. 'We're running out of time, Fitch.'

Dark circles had formed under Peter's eyes, mirroring Fitch's own tiredness. His face is haggard and lined, the wrinkles appearing deeper as he rubs his temples in frustration and worry.

'Tell me about Lister,' Fitch inquired, pulling up a chair with an earnest glance. 'I didn't get involved when all that stuff kicked off a couple of years back. That said, everything I've heard about him tells me he's a bad 'un.'

Peter took a deep breath in as he prepared to tell Fitch about his former boss. 'Lister was as sharp as a tack in his heyday. He rose through the ranks from a fresh-faced constable like a hot knife through butter,' Peter began, his voice tinged with admiration and regret. 'I was green as grass when I first met him. He was Chief Inspector then and took me under his wing.'

Fitch unfolded his arms, his tone gentle yet insistent. 'Where did everything go wrong for Lister?' he prodded, sensing that the turning point of this tale was crucial to understanding the entire story. The poorly lit room held its breath as the question hung in mid-air, waiting for an answer to unravel the mystery.

'It began with a case of counterfeit money flooding Suffolk like a mischievous stream.'

Fitch moved position onto the other side of the door-frame, arms folded again. 'And Lister was behind it?'

'Indeed. But the clever sod pinned it on a junior officer, a scapegoat so green you could have mistaken him for a blade of grass. It was a masterstroke.'

'No one caught up with Lister?'

Peter grinned, then the smile faded. 'I did, except I couldn't prove anything. He knew that and threatened to frame me the next time if I said anything.'

'And you didn't?'

'No, and I regret my cowardice to this day,' Peter said in a sad tone. 'Oh, I convinced myself it wasn't my fault, and he had the power. But I knew he had me exactly where he wanted me.'

'So, what happened?'

'The young copper got the sack. Lister got a promotion from chief inspector to commander, and with that power he had me reassigned to Stanton Parva.'

Fitch's mouth fell open at the revelations. 'So that's how you came to our little corner of Norfolk?'

As a small smile played across Peter's lips, he shifted uncomfortably in his seat. 'To be honest,' he began, his voice tinged with bitterness, 'I despised everything about the wretched place. Small-minded villagers and stuck in the middle of nowhere. He spoke with disdain in his voice. The memories brought him no joy.

'And now?'

Peter's lips curled upward into a sly smile. His eyes sparkled with mischief as he revealed his true feelings about the village and its inhabitants. 'To be completely honest, I wouldn't want to be anywhere else.'

'Interesting stuff, but I agree. What's your plan?'

'The problem is, we have between now...,' Peter looked at the standard issue wall clock just above Fitch's head. 'That's 10.30 pm, and noon tomorrow. My strategy is to leave Ant and Lyn out of it from now on in. Heaven knows they need some peace before the big day.'

Fitch looked astonished. 'Just how do you intend to do that?'

Peter gave his friend an icy stare. 'I'll lie to them if I must. If I don't catch Lister in the next twelve hours, I'm going to tell Ant and Lyn he's in custody.'

'Are you mad?' Fitch looked astonished at Peter's admission.

'Do you have a better idea? They won't postpone the

wedding—and I understand their reasons. However, what's the point of them looking over their shoulders every two seconds? If anything will ruin their day, that will.'

'But aren't you leaving yourself wide open, not just to criticism if Lister carries out his threat,' Fitch began. 'Whether he succeeds won't be the point. You'll get the blame? You know, the sack, lose your pension. At worse, you end up in prison. Now, wouldn't that be ironic?'

'That's a chance I'm prepared to take. They stuck their necks out for me two years ago. You might remember we weren't close then. In fact, Ant and I detested one another. They didn't have to get involved, but they saved my career, and offered friendship into the bargain. I won't turn my back on them now, whatever the cost to me.'

Fitch shook his head again. 'If someone suggested what's going on as a plot for a book, their publisher would send them packing with a flee in their ear.'

'Except this isn't fiction, and our villain isn't make believe,' said Peter.

'Like a fox with a thorn in its paw,' Peter nodded, swivelling to face the window where the moonlight played shadow puppets among the stacks of files. 'He blames them entirely for his ruination—their cunning and their refusal to be intimidated by his rank or reputation.'

'Any man who holds a grudge that tightly is bound to squeeze out some nasty plans,' Fitch stated, his voice carrying a tinge of warning and concern. A sense of unease settled over the room, mirroring the tension radiating off Fitch's body.

'He's had plenty of time to stew in his own venomous thoughts,' Peter sighed, feeling the pressure of the impending nuptials press upon him. 'Those two are like rabbits cheerfully hopping along, not knowing where the snare will snap shut.'

'Then we best find that snare before they stumble into it,' said Fitch, determination lighting his eyes.

'So, you're with me, even though you're Anthony's Best Man?'

Fitch's response was immediate, without the slightest hesitation. His voice rang out with conviction and trust as he replied, 'I trust you completely, 100%.' There was no doubt in his mind as he uttered the words. He knew that the bond between them was unbreakable. Even in the face of uncertainty and danger, Fitch had full faith in his companion, a testament to their deep and unwavering friendship.

Friday, 5th September: 9.30 pm

IAN LISTER PAUSED beneath the gnarled branches of an ancient oak, his breath misting in the cool evening air. The once formidable commander moved with a predatory stealth that defied his years, each step calculated to avoid detection. His eyes, sharp and unyielding, scanned the quaint cottages where Lyn had sought refuge. He knew her habits; he watched, waited, and plotted every conceivable move.

'Predictable,' he murmured as he spied the flicker of light in the windows of the Blackthorn residence. 'Tea at nine, just like clockwork.'

With a cunning grin, he removed a small listening device from his pocket - a trinket he had stolen during one of his well-planned reconnaissance trips. He had placed them strategically around the village, and Stanton Hall, ensuring that no whisper or footstep would go unnoticed. Lister played the role of ghost to perfection. He haunted Ant and Lyn's every move. Present but not present, orchestrating fear with the finesse of a maestro.

Meanwhile, inside the warm glow of her cottage, Lyn attempted to focus on the wedding. Usually the epitome of calm, a headteacher well-versed in managing chaos. However, on this night, her hands trembled as she fidgeted with the accessories she's chosen for her wedding dress. Tina, Lyn's school secretary and close friend, watched her with concern.

'Maybe it's time to call it a night. You've a busy day tomorrow from the crack of dawn. Don't forget we're at the hairdressers at seven-thirty,' she suggests gently, reaching out to still her fidgeting fingers. 'You've done enough.'

Lyn attempted a smile, her lips tugging upward in a facsimile of her usual easy-going demeanour. 'I'm fine, Tina. Just rattled. Thank you for agreeing to stay the night with me. I—.'

'Don't say another word,' Tina answered, her reassuring smile helping her close friend and colleague to relax a little. 'Let's try some of that mindfulness meditation you're always on about,' Tina suggested with a hopeful chuckle, trying to inject a note of levity into the tension that surrounded the bride to be.

'Mindfulness against a murderer,' Lyn quipped dryly, though her heart wasn't in it.

They settled onto the sofa, attempting to synchronise their breathing with the guided voice emanating from Lyn's mobile. Instead of finding peace, Lyn's thoughts drifted to the dark corners of the room, where shadows played tricks on her mind. Every whisper of wind against the windowpane felt like the breath of a vengeful spectre.

'Tina,' she whispered after a moment, her voice barely audible over the soothing tones of the meditation guide, 'Do you ever wonder if Ant and I will ever be free of him?'

'I do,' she replied, her voice steady despite her own doubts. 'But you've both faced down his worst before, haven't you? You'll do it again.'

Friday, 5th September: 9.30 pm

PETER THUMBED through the tattered pages of his address book, eyes flicking back and forth in search of a lead that might have slipped through the cracks. Fitch hovered over his shoulder like an inquisitive sparrow, peering at the scribbled notes and crossed-out numbers.

'Anything?' Fitch asked, his voice edged with hope.

'Still trying,' Peter muttered.

'Maybe Phyllis has heard something,' Peter suggested, half-heartedly. 'Though I might as well interrogate the ducks down at the village pond for all the reliable intelligence she provides.'

'Her network is... extensive though,' Fitch chimed in, ever the optimist despite past wild goose chases—sometimes literally.

'Right, 'extensive," Peter echoed with a smile, reaching for the phone with the same trepidation one might reserve for a venomous serpent.

Before he dialled her number, his office 'phone rang out.

'I have Betty on the line for you, Sir. Should I put her through?'

Peter looked at Fitch with amazement. 'Er, yes. Of course.'

87

'Betty?' Fitch mouthed, matching Peter's look of utter surprise.'

'Dear Inspector. Is that you?' Betty's voice barely reached Peter's ear, so thin and muted.'

'Yes... Yes, I'm here Betty. How may I help?'

'I apologise for ringing you at this late hour.'

'Not at all. Is everything all right?'

Betty paused for a few seconds. 'With me? Oh, yes, I'm fine. In fact, I'm more than fine. You see, Phyllis has gone home, so I'm free to speak.'

'Oh, dear. So, there is something wrong?'

'Not at all,' Betty chuckled. 'You see, the only time I get to speak properly to anyone is when Phyllis isn't with me. Don't get me wrong, I love her dearly and we've been insep-arable friends since infant school. The only trouble...well... I'm sure you've noticed she can be a bit well...forthright with her opinions. I don't mind really, but on this occasion, I wanted to speak to you directly. Is that OK?'

It took all of Peter's reserve not to chuckle at Betty's dilemma. His restraint not helped one bit by the tears of silent laughter rolling down Fitch's cheeks.

'Oh, most certainly, Betty,' Peter said earnestly, while averting his gaze from the village mechanic. 'Do I take it you have information for me?'

'Actually, yes, I do. You see, there was a man,' she began as Peter felt his pulse quicken. 'A rather dashing man in a brooding sort of way. He asked about the old lodge house to the Cunningham Estate.'

'Did he now?' Peter's voice sharpened with interest as he scribbled down the details. 'When was this, Betty?'

'Why, just this afternoon? I'd taken some home-baked bread to old Mrs Trotter up by Gallows Bend when he misjudged the curve coming the other way and fell off his bicycle. Of course, once I'd got over the shock, I rendered what help I could to the poor man. He was ever so gracious, and we got into polite conversation. That's when he asked me about the Gatehouse. He asked if I knew if it was for rent. I thought nothing of it. But it's been troubling me ever since...you know, with everything else that's been going on.'

Fitch wasn't laughing anymore. He hung on the Betty's every word, as did Peter.

'That's Lister to a tee. Can charm the birds out of a tree when the mood takes him,' Peter said while holding his hand over the microphone of the telephone receiver.

'Yes... Yes, I'm still here,' Peter assured Betty. 'Tell me, who else knows about this?'

Betty looked thoughtful. 'Well, er, no one, I suppose. You won't tell Phyllis, will you? She'd be furious not to have been the one to tell you.'

'Not at all, Betty. I understand what you're saying,' Peter said in a reassuring tone. 'Thank you and keep your eyes peeled. Don't approach him though if you see him again.'

'Of course, dear. I'll be as discreet as a fox in a henhouse!' she promised, clearly missing the irony of her own analogy.

After exchanging goodbyes, Peter hung up, the sense of urgency tangible. The wedding day loomed like storm clouds over the Norfolk Broads, each tick of the clock, a stark reminder of the danger shadowing the soon-to-be-wed couple.

'Sounds like a solid lead,' Fitch said, peering at Peter's notes with renewed interest.

'Or another red herring,' Peter countered, 'But there's no time for doubt. We must act on it now.'

'Let's go then,' Fitch said.

Friday, 5th September: 10.00 pm

PETER AND FITCH saw two small, square gate-lodges and a pair of worn, intricate, wrought-iron gates.

A cloudless night allowed the moon's soft glow to kiss everything it touched, making the scene reminiscent of a Hammer House of Horror movie from the 1950s.

Peter trod cautiously as he approached the lodge to the left of the once magnificent entrance. To his right stood the half-demolished remains of the other lodge.

'Watch out, Peter,' Fitch cautioned as the detective pushed on the half-open front door of the small lodge. 'If he's inside, he'll be ready for you.'

Fitch hovered behind, a silent presence offering both support and caution as Peter stepped into the dimly lit room. The moon's silvery fingers reached through grime-covered windows, painting everything in a ghostly hue.

Peter heard Fitch's warning, but was too immersed in his task to acknowledge the alert. The odour of mildew and abandonment was overwhelming. Shadows clung to walls like cobwebs as Peter's flashlight swept across the tiny interior.

A floorboard creaked under Peter's weight as he advanced further into the lodge, his eyes scanning every corner for any sign of movement.

'Looks like nobody's home,' Fitch quipped, though his voice lacked its usual mirth.

'Can't be,' Peter muttered, more to himself than his companion. His mind raced—Betty's tip couldn't have been, could it?

The men navigated the cluttered floor, each step threw

up clouds of dust that waltzed lazily in the beams of their flashlights. Outside, all remained silent, save for the distant hoot of an owl. The creature mocked them from the safety of the dark canopy of trees that lay in the near distance.

'Over there,' Fitch nodded towards a flimsy door leading to the kitchen. 'If he's here, it's his only place left to hide.'

'Damn it,' Peter exhales sharply as he flung the door opened with such force that it broke apart, his disappointment palpable. 'He's not here.'

Peter scratched his earlobe, the tension visible in the tight lines of his face. Then, his eyes caught on something— a piece of paper pinned to the wall with a solitary, rusty nail. He approached and pulled the note free.

'Hello, Peter,' he read aloud, the words crawling under his skin like ants. 'Sorry to miss our little reunion. Save me a slice of wedding cake, won't you? - Ian.'

Peter's heart raced as he read the chilling note left by his deadly foe. The empty lodge now felt like a trap, the surrounding silence heavier than ever before. Fitch's expression mirrored Peter's unease. The humour drained from his features.

The detective crumpled the note in his hand, his jaw clenched in frustration. Ian Lister was playing games, toying with them like prey in a cat-and-mouse chase. The stakes had never been higher, and the sense of danger loomed like a heavy fog in the deserted lodge.

'Cheeky sod,' Fitch growled, peering over Peter's shoulder.

'There's the proof he strung Betty along. Of course, he didn't know who he'd come across. What he knew was whoever he told, they'd relay the suspicious sighting to me.'

In a moment suspended in time, the two men stood amidst the ruins of what might have been their greatest victory, now turned to ash. Silence filled the space, save for a whisper of the wind falling lazily through a broken window.

'Let's get to the village,' Peter said, unfolding the crumpled note and tucking it into his pocket. 'He's getting closer and watching us right now.'

As they left the abandoned lodge to its ghosts, the moonlit landscape appeared to watch expectantly. The steeple of Stanton Parva's ancient church pierced the clear night sky. It served as an unwitting beacon for the storm that gathered pace with each passing minute.

And as they slipped back into the police car, a feeling of unease settled deep within the men's bones. With so little time left, Peter knew Lister had the upper hand.

Chapter Eight

A WATCHING MOON

SATURDAY, *6th September: The Wedding Day; 1.30 am*

Peter stood in the sombre silence of his back garden, the full moon casting a silver sheen over the dewy blades of grass. He squinted at the glowing screen of his mobile—1:30 am, a ridiculous hour for anyone with less weighty concerns. But sleep? Not while Lister remained at large. A solitary owl hooted its lonesome serenade, and the distant bark of a fox offered little comfort.

Crisp air bit at his cheeks as he tilted his head back, eyes tracing the constellations scattered across the ink-black canvas above. The stars were as indifferent as they were eternal, silent observers to earthbound follies. Peter wondered about the countless dramas they'd witnessed through the ages. Feasts of victory, the wails of despair—and how insignificant the worries of one small village might seem in the grand tapestry of time.

Yet, here he stood, very much entangled in the affairs of the village, alone with the weight of a looming disaster. The moon, an unblinking sentinel, stared back at him, and he fixated on its cratered visage. It reminded him, unhelpfully, of Lister—the man whose slippery nature had eluded Peter's grasp just when capture seemed imminent.

'Missed him at the Gate Lodge,' he muttered under his breath, a private admonition. 'Could've had him.' His mind replayed the scene, each error magnified, each decision second-guessed. The wedding of Ant and Lyn loomed like a ticking bomb, and Peter couldn't shake the sense that he's the one holding the detonator.

He paced a small circle, hands stuffed into the pockets of his work jacket, as if physical movement could shake loose a solution from the recesses of his brain. Lister's Spectre danced mockingly around the edges of his thoughts —a crazed marionette pulling strings of doubt and fear.

'Should've been simple,' Peter chided himself, scowling at the moon as if it were an accomplice to his frustrations. 'Catch the villain, save the day, all before the 'I dos.' Instead, a tangled mess, the prospect of what calamity might unfold threatened to consume him.

'No one deserves this,' he whispered, a plea tossed into the void. How would he face the Earl of Stanton? The man's loyalty to the village was as sturdy as the ancient oaks dotting his estate. Peter dreaded the thought of the ramifications of failing to protect his son and future daughter-in-law.

'Norfolk's supposed to be peaceful,' he scoffed quietly, shaking his head. 'Not harbouring villains with a penchant for wedding day murder.'

But there was no escaping the truth. Peter knew that Lister's shadow stretched far beyond the confines of the garden. It reached into the village itself, threatening their idyllic life with the sort of excitement none of them desired.

'Time's running out,' he said to no one, a mantra that did nothing to still his racing heart. The stakes were too high, the risk too daunting. And yet, surrounded by the silent majesty of the Norfolk landscape, under the watchful gaze of the celestial audience, Peter felt helpless.

The full moon continued to hang above, indifferent to human affairs. It cast its silvery gaze upon the carefully tended flower beds and the dew-laden grass. In just a few hours, he'd face Ant and Lyn. The impending nuptials set to fuel village gossip—if Lister didn't upstage the day with his own brand of mayhem.

Each tick of an unseen clock anchored him to the spot. To lie to his friends, to assure them that Lister was securely behind bars, when in fact the man was as elusive as the morning mist—that's the plan. It gnawed at Peter's conscience, yet he steeled himself against the onslaught of doubt. 'For their peace of mind,' he whispered into the night, trying to convince the owls and the foxes...and himself.

But the tranquillity of the scene betrayed the turmoil within. He shivered, not from the cool night air, but from the potential consequences of his actions. If things went awry, it wouldn't just be his career finished; the trust of every villager, from the Earl and Countess of Stanton to the gossiping Phyllis, would crumble into dust.

As the grim thoughts churned through his mind, a rustling sound sliced through the silence, jarring Peter from his despair. Instinctively, he crouched, heart hammering against his ribcage. Could it be Lister, emerging from the shadows to exact vengeance?

Eyes darting, Peter scanned the darkness for anything that could serve as a makeshift weapon. His hand closed around a stone recently unearthed from a gardening project. The rock's cool, solid presence in his grip offered a morsel of comfort.

Time stretched taut as he prepared for confrontation, muscles tensed and ready to spring. But then, as suddenly as it appeared, the tension shattered, leaving Peter blinking in bewilderment. A black cat, sleek and unconcerned, sauntered across the lawn, its tail flicking in mild annoyance. Peter exhaled a shaky laugh, feeling foolish, and tossed the stone aside. The only threat tonight came on silent paws with a penchant for midnight prowling.

'Lucky you're not Lister,' he muttered to the retreating feline, whose only response was a disdainful glance over its shoulder. The encounter, absurd as it is, did little to ease the knot in Peter's stomach.

He returned his gaze to the moon, the unchanged and unchanging guardian of the night sky. It offered no counsel, no hint of what the dawn might bring. All Peter could do was wait and hope that when the sun rose over Norfolk's muted fields, it brought with it a day free of calamity and full of celebration.

'Stanton Parva deserves a day off from drama,' he said to himself, trying to infuse a touch of humour into the situation. The owl hooted in a distant tree, as though in agreement, and for a moment, Peter allowed himself the luxury of a smile.

Peter's gaze drifts skyward once again, the moon hanging like an unblinking eye over Stanton Parva. It bathed the garden in a silver glow, a silent sentinel to his inner turmoil. He sought some spark of wisdom, some celestial sign, but found none. The moon remained indifferent to human affairs, a constant in the ever-shifting tides of life below.

'Could use that calmness,' he whispered.

His thoughts, unbidden, tumble backward in time to the day he first met Ant and Lyn. He had been official and cold then, the barrier of his badge between them. Ant had squared up to him, eyes flashing with that characteristic blend of arrogance and challenge. 'We're just trying to help,' Ant had insisted, as Peter fixed him with a sceptical glare.

'Help?' Peter had scoffed. 'By trampling over a crime scene?'

It was Lyn who had stepped forward, her voice the soothing balm to Ant's fiery presence. 'Peter, we know this is your jurisdiction. We respect that. But we might have seen something you need.'

He'd wanted to dismiss them outright, these two civilians who dared to encroach on police matters. Yet there was something about Lyn's earnest appeal, the genuine concern in her eyes, that had stayed his hand. Even now, the memory of it softened the hard lines of his face.

'Peacemaker Lyn,' he murmured fondly into the stillness. How quickly she had found her way past his defences, guiding Ant to do the same. And now, he couldn't imagine tackling a case—or the oddities of Stanton Parva—without them.

'Trust Lyn to smooth over ruffled feathers,' he reflected. If only she could soothe the doubts as easily. But tonight, it wasn't just ruffled feathers at stake. It was the safety of everyone he held dear from the spectre of Lister's grievance.

'Guess I could use some peace-making magic myself,' Peter conceded, his chuckle lost to the owl's call. He could almost hear Lyn's reassuring response, a lighthouse beacon cutting through the fog of his uncertainty.

'Come on, Peter,' he goads himself, straightening his

shoulders. 'Dawn will come, and with it, action.' The moon offered no reply. Somewhere in the back of his mind, he clung to the hope that when push came to shove, he'd find the right words to say. For now, though, the night held its breath, waiting alongside Peter for the morning's light.

Peter's thoughts drifted to another case, as if the moon above were a silent witness beckoning him to reflect on past times as a tonic for the present. The entrepreneur in his boathouse on Stanton Broad—another mystery that Ant and Lyn had stumbled upon before him. He remembered arriving at the scene. The aftertaste of their eagerness still lingered, an invisible barrier to his own investigative instincts.

'Always one step behind,' he muttered to himself with a rueful shake of his head. The resentment that once simmered within him felt distant now, like the echoes of footsteps down a long, empty corridor. Peter had despised the ease of Ant's life—the privilege, the comfort. The doors open wide without a knock. It was a stark contrast to his own upbringing. One painted in shades of scrimping and saving, of a mother's weary sighs as she juggled jobs to keep them all fed.

'Could've used a bit of that silver spoon myself,' he whispered, the words barely louder than the rustle of leaves underfoot. It was a sentiment drenched in the sourness of old envy, but now tempered by the warmth of something akin to gratitude. Gratitude for the friendship that had grown, despite—or perhaps because of—their differences.

He recalled his father, a man of few words and even fewer displays of affection—a hard man worn down by life's relentless grind. But there were those fleeting moments, rare and raw, when his father's stoic mask would slip. At such times, a vulnerability Peter could never quite reconcile with the gruff exterior emerged. A child couldn't fathom the depths of their parents' trials, he realised, not until they'd waded through their own.

'Life's funny,' Peter mused to the indifferent stars. 'Just when you think you've got it all figured out...' His voice trailed off into the night, unfinished thoughts scattering like dandelion seeds in the wind.

The shrill cry of his mobile alarm suddenly shattered the silence. Peter's heart leapt into a frenetic dance, pounding against his ribs in protest. The deadline he'd set for himself loomed large now, casting a shadow over the dawn that crept ever closer with every passing second.

'Decision time,' he whispered, the humour in his tone doing little to dissipate the tension. Lie or tell the truth? The question hung like a pendulum swinging between honour and necessity. At 9:00 am, he'd be calling Ant and Lyn, and the words he chose would shape the day—for better or worse.

Peter's pulse quickened, a frantic rhythm that seemed to resonate with the distant call of wildlife. He wiped his clammy forehead with the back of his hand and squinted at the moon as if it held the answer. His stomach churned, and for a moment he feared he'd collapse.

'Stop it,' he murmured to himself, though his voice sounded more like a plea than a command.

The quiet of the night did nothing to soothe his nerves. The closer the hands of an unseen clock crept towards dawn, the heavier the weight of deceit pressed upon him. Fitch's words echoed in his mind—a solemn promise to stay silent. Yet, Peter couldn't help but question the ethics of dragging his friend into his web of lies.

'Trust goes both ways, Fitch,' he had said, seeking reassurance in the man's steady gaze. 'You won't breathe a word?'

'Cross my heart,' was the reply, but now, alone with his doubts, Peter wondered if he'd compromised them both. How could he expect Fitch to betray years of loyalty to Ant and Lyn? A shiver ran down his spine—not from the cold, but from fear of unravelling friendships.

'I wish I could disappear right now?' he sighed, half-expecting the universe to offer a secret trapdoor beneath his feet.

His thoughts drifted back to his childhood again. The comforting embrace of his mother's kitchen in the family's tiny, terraced house. A smell of fresh bread making his current nausea even more poignant. He longed for the simplicity of childhood, where the worst of his troubles smothered in flour-dusted hugs and the warmth of a just-baked loaf.

'Bit late for that, Peter,' he chided himself, tucking away those tender memories alongside the resolve he knew he must muster.

In Stanton Parva, as stars twinkled like mischievous eyes overhead, Peter braced for the morning's revelations. His only armour, hope that his choice, however flawed, might still protect his friends, and the village he regarded as home.

Peter pivoted on the balls of his feet, a restless sentry in his own back garden, as his gazed remained fixed on the moon. Its cratered face hung in the sky like an omnipresent guardian—or a silent judge. He tried to anchor his thoughts on anything but Lister, yet his mind, a traitor to his will, looped back to the man with the constancy of a broken record.

'Come on, Peter, get a grip,' he muttered, scratching the back of his neck where a prickling sense of unease had taken up residence. But it was no use; the lunar glow threw his fears into stark relief, painting the night in shades of doubt and dread.

Lister loomed in his thoughts, an unwelcome spectre at this nocturnal hour. The moon, indifferent and unchanging, seemed to reflect his own powerlessness—a mirror to the ebb and flow of anxiety within him. Just as the sea ebbed and flowed to the moon's embrace, so too was Peter, ensnared by the gravity of his nemesis' potential for chaos.

'Steady on,' he coached himself, trying to shake off the feeling that he'd lost control. But the semblance of calm was short-lived as a sudden chill cascaded down his spine, startling him with its intensity.

It was as though the very air around him had shifted; the temperature plummeting with the imagined cackle of Lister's malevolence. For a split second, Peter's mind conjured the visage of his adversary in place of the moon, smirking down at him with cold amusement. The notion was ludicrous; he knew—yet the shiver that skittered across his skin felt all too real.

'You've got to stop this,' he chided himself, but his heart drummed a frantic rhythm against his ribs, betraying his attempts at nonchalance. It was as if Lister wasn't just a man but a malevolent presence that had seeped into the very fabric of Stanton Parva, inescapable as the moon's ghostly light.

Peter's feet sank into the dew-heavy grass as he retreated from the garden's edge, where moonlight has pooled like spilt milk. His hands were deep in his pockets, fists clenched around the scant warmth they found there. The night was still, save for the rustling whispers of nocturnal creatures and his own wavering breaths.

He should be inside, buried under a duvet, not out here

wrestling with shadows and doubts. But sleep was a stranger these days, and Peter paced the length of his garden like a restless spirit, every footstep an echo of unease.

The house loomed before him, its windows darkened, eyes in the pale face of dawn. He should go in, he knew it. Instead, he paused at the back door, hand hovering over the handle, heart thumping a staccato rhythm. It was absurd to fear entering one's own home, yet fear it he did—not of what lay within, but of Lister's next move, a spectre hanging over him, unseen yet palpable.

With a shaky exhale, Peter stepped inside and quietly closed the door behind him. He leaned against the solid door, allowing the relative warmth of the house to seep into his chilled bones.

He allowed the silence to envelop him, a blanket woven from the threads of his solitude. The ticking of the hallway clock was a comforting heartbeat, steady and reassuring in its constancy. But comfort was a luxury Peter couldn't afford, not when each tick marked the approach of an inevitable confrontation.

In the dim light, photographs smiled down at him from the walls, a collage of happier times. He fixated on one of Ant and Lyn, arms around each other, eyes alight with shared secrets and laughter. The sight twisted into something deep within him, and he turned away. The image burned into his retinas.

As he did so, something caught his eye in the semi-darkness. Peter hesitated. Were his senses playing tricks on him again? He couldn't put his finger on it, but something in that room had changed.

'Morning, Detective Inspector Riley'. The calm, muted voice shattered Peter. He knew at one to whom the voice belonged.

'So, you've finally come?' Peter said in an equally calm voice. In a curious way, Peter had hoped for this moment. All the tension, fear, and guilt melted away as his training kicked in. But it wasn't only about his training. He'd wanted, even needed, to come face to face with the man who threatened everything he held important.

The shadowy figure seated in an armchair with his back to the curtained window offered mocking laughter. 'You didn't think my brief visit is just for that fool toff and his teacher girlfriend, did you?'

'Who knows what's in that twisted head of yours?' Peter began. 'To be truthful, I don't have the slightest interest in playing your game. Just know this. I will not allow you to hurt anyone today, or any other day.'

Lister let out a deep roar of laughter that echoed around the sparsely furnished room.

Peter's heart pounded as he faced off against Lister, the disgraced Chief Inspector, in the dimly lit room. The tension crackled, their eyes locked in a silent battle of wills. Peter's training kicked in as he assessed the situation, his mind clear and focused.

Without warning, Lister lunged forward, aiming to overpower Peter with his strength. But Peter was ready. He sidestepped Lister's attack and delivered a swift blow to Lister's side. The impact reverberated through the room, and Lister staggered back, momentarily stunned.

Seizing the opportunity, Peter moved with lightning speed. He lunged forward, tackling Lister to the ground. They grappled for control, each fighting for their own survival. Peter's muscles strained against Lister's powerful resistance, but he refused to give in.

As they rolled on the floor, knocking over furniture and scattering photographs, Peter's determination grew stronger.

He knew that everything he held dear was at stake—Ant and Lyn's safety and his own sense of justice.

With a surge of strength, Peter pinned Lister down, his knee pressing against Lister's chest. He could feel Lister's laboured breaths beneath him, a testament to their gruelling struggle. Sweat dripped down Peter's forehead as he looked into Lister's defiant eyes.

'You thought you could break us,' Peter growled through gritted teeth. 'But we are stronger than you ever imagined.'

Lister let out a mocking laugh. His eyes glinted with a twisted satisfaction that sent a shiver down Peter's spine. With one swift move, Lister twisted his body and freed himself from Peter's grip.

The struggle resumed with renewed ferocity, but Peter refused to back down. He summoned every ounce of strength he had left and charged toward Lister, tackling him once again. The room echoed with the sound of furniture crashing around them.

Their struggle raged on, each exchange of blows fuelling their determination. It was a battle for survival, a battle against darkness and evil. Bruised, Peter fought with a determination that burned deep within him.

Finally, with one last surge of strength, Peter overpowered Lister. He pinned him down with all his might, their faces inches apart. The room fell silent, save for their ragged breaths and the pounding of Peter's heart.

Lister's eyes flickered with defeat. With his victory secured, Peter looked around the room at the battered remnants of a once secluded refuge. The walls bore witness to their struggle, capturing the intensity and sheer willpower that had brought him to this moment.

As he stood there, triumphant yet weary, Peter knew this

struggle was not just about protecting his friends or seeking justice.

And in that moment of clarity amidst the chaos, Peter found a renewed sense of purpose. Ant and Lyn were safe. He'd no need to lie to his best friends about Lister's capture. Yet something tugged at his consciousness. His beaten foe had said nothing he did could stop what was coming. Had he tasted victory too early?

Chapter Nine

SHADOWS OF CHAOS

Saturday, 6th September: 6.30 am

PETER'S HEART raced with urgency. In his lounge, he swiftly restrained Lister with one hand and tried to operate his mobile with the other. His fingers, slippery with the sheen of exertion, danced across the screen, summoning police backup and Fitch with a succession of swift taps.

'Tell me, Lister!' Peter growled, not easing the pressure on the restrained man beneath him. 'What have you done to disrupt the wedding?'

Lister's chuckle was as infuriating as a wasp at a picnic. 'Oh, Peter, always so direct,' he taunted from his prone position. 'You really think I'd orchestrate someone's demise without a helping hand? There's nothing you can do to stop what will happen today.'

The threat hung between them like a cobweb in the corner of an otherwise pristine room. Lister stubbornly held onto his secrets, even under Peter's relentless questioning.

As if on cue, the cavalry arrived. Officers poured into the house with the efficiency of ants discovering a spilt spot of jam. They took Peter out of the wrestling match and cuffed Lister's wrists. The officers understood the situation and nodded with determined expressions. As they hauled Lister to his feet, Peter issued his commands with the solemnity of a captain addressing his crew.

'Keep your eyes glued to that man,' he ordered, pointing at Lister. 'He can be very manipulative. Do not speak to him. If he attempts to say anything to anyone, use your imagination within the law to stop him.'

Understanding the gravity of the situation, the officers nodded, their expressions serious. Lister left the house with all the pomp and circumstance of a fallen dignitary, his head held high despite his ignominious defeat.

'Take him straight to the station,' Peter continued, 'And throw the man in a cell. Not a word between you, hear? Silence is golden, especially with this one.'

The officers affirmed with curt nods, their silence already forming an impenetrable barrier around the master manipulator. The police van's doors slammed shut with a definitive thud, sealing Lister away from the world he sought to unsettle. As the vehicle retreated down the lane, its presence faded until only the birdsong remained, as though even the countryside exhaled in relief.

Peter watched the police van disappear around the bend, taking the enigmatic Lister with it. Despite the early hour, the day seemed to have already unfurled its fair share of chaos before most villagers had even stirred from their slumber.

As he stepped back into the house, Peter's mind raced through the events that had led to this moment. The threat of disruption loomed over the upcoming wedding. Lister's cryptic words only added to the sense of.

With a heavy sigh, Peter rubbed a hand over his tired face. He knew that there was still much to do to ensure the safety and success of the wedding.

Taking a deep breath, Peter squared his shoulders and turned his attention to the task at hand. With steely determination in his eyes. The moment was cool and sweet, but the taste of Lister's insinuations lingered, leaving a bitter note amidst the pastoral peace.

A few minutes later, the sound of Fitch's rattling Land Rover pierced the quiet. Peter recognised the engine sound and stood at the open front door to welcome his visitor.

Fitch launched himself up the pathway, his face contorted with concern. Peter shook his hand and showed him into the lounge.

'Heavens,' Fitch said, surveying a scene of disarray. Cushions askew, a potted plant forlorn on its side, and the evidence of a scuffle etched into the carpet's disrupted pile. 'Blimey, Peter, what sort of ruckus did you have here?' Fitch exclaimed.

Peter wiped his brow, the tension from recent events still palpable. 'Lister,' he began, his voice heavy with fatigue and determination. 'He's even more conniving than we expected.'

Fitch frowned as he took in Peter's words. 'That man is a bad one,' he muttered, his eyes scanning the room for any lingering signs of trouble.

As Peter recounted the details of the morning's chaos, Fitch listened intently, his expression shifting from shock to outrage. 'We can't let him get away with this,' Fitch declared, his fists clenched at his sides. 'The wedding must go on without a hitch, no matter what Lister tries to throw our way.'

Peter grunted. 'Lister's intent on carrying out his plan. My concern is he's laid such a devious plan that it won't matter that he's behind bars. That's what he hinted at, anyway.'

'All the same,' Fitch began. 'Well done on the arrest, mate. I hope you told your officers to throw the key away.'

'If only,' Peter replied.

Fitch raised an eyebrow. 'He could try it on. Attempting to intimidate you into making a mistake...or worse, forcing Ant and Lyn to call the wedding off, even at this late stage.'

'Normally I'd agree,' Peter countered, shaking his head. 'But Lister's never been one for dirtying his own hands. He prefers to pull the strings from afar. And there's something else. The trouble is, I can't put my finger on it.'

'What do you mean?'

'I dunno,' began Peter. 'But I have a horrible feeling I've missed a detail. The back of my brain tells me I saw something that I thought at the time might be of importance. The trouble is, I didn't make a record of whatever it was. Now I can't place it, but I know it'll come back to haunt me if I don't bottom it out.'

Fitch stared at the detective, not knowing what to say.

After several seconds of reflective silence, Peter roused himself. 'Listen, I need you to do me a favour. Can you contact Ant and Lyn for me? Tell them the news about Lister being behind bars, but leave out the rest. They deserve to enjoy their day without this hanging over them.'

'Of course,' Fitch nodded, his face etched with an earnest expression. 'I'll keep it light. Just the arrest and nothing more.'

'Good man. Meanwhile, I've got some loose ends to tie up. Need to make sure today goes off without a hitch—or at least with no more hitches than a wedding usually includes.'

They share a brief chuckle before stepping out onto Peter's front path, the early sun casting long shadows across the dew-speckled lawn. They parted ways with a handshake. Fitch headed toward the joyful cacophony of wedding preparations. Peter set off to ensure the safety of the blissfully unaware couple.

The village stirred. Quaint thatched roofs and cobblestone streets basked in the glow of the new day. The rolling Norfolk landscape stretched out beyond; a testament to the serene beauty that belay the undercurrents of intrigue woven through the fabric of the village.

As Peter made his way through the village, his mind turned over the cryptic puzzle Lister had presented. He knew he had to unravel the mystery before the consequences shattered the community.

Passing by the village green, he spotted Phyllis speaking animatedly with the baker. The early morning sun painted a golden hue over their figures. Phylis' eager expression and the baker's efforts to untangle himself from the encounter and get on with the day's deliveries. Approaching the pair, Peter wished the odd couple a cheery morning.

'Phyllis was quick to spot her favourite policeman. 'Hello to you, too. Have you caught the rascal yet?'

Her question posed a dilemma for Peter. Admit to Lister's arrest and set a hare running through the village. Deny contact with the villain and risk fear and trepidation running riot. The source of both scenarios stood in front of him, with the baker seizing his opportunity to slip away.

The detective offered a third play. 'Funny you should mention that. Lister boarded a train for London late last night. I've not heard from the Metropolitan Police yet, but I hope to do so shortly. Now I know you will keep this a secret, won't you, Phyllis?'

'Assuredly,' beamed the elderly lady, her hat sitting atop her swept back hair at an odd angle. 'You can rely on me, er, Peter. I can call you Peter, can't I? Your secret is safe with me. Anyway, I must be going. Betty has a slight sniffle, so I said I'd pick her up some Vicks Vapour Rub to ease her chest.'

Peter smiled as he watched Phyllis walk briskly toward the chemist, whose opening hour had not yet arrived. 'It'll be all over the village within thirty minutes,' he mused to himself.

Peter doubled back on himself and strolled up the high street and into the hallowed halls of Stanton Parva's church. His gaze swept over the pews and altar, adorned with flowers that trumpeted joy and celebration. But today it played an odd symphony today. One played to the rhythm of sniffer dogs and officers in muted tones, their presence a blunt contrast to the bright chrysanthemums and dainty roses.

Hushed murmurs and the occasional shuffling of feet filled the church as Peter made his way towards the subdued group of officers. He spotted the reverend Morton standing at the altar. The cleric bent forward in solemn prayer, oblivious to the activities that surrounded him within the sacred space.

Approaching his officers, Peter spoke in a hushed tone. 'What's the situation?' he asked. The constables exchanged uneasy glances before one of them, a young officer with a freckled face, spoke up. 'Sir, we've swept the church twice, and searched the entire village. Clean as a whistle,' he reported,

Peter nodded, rubbing his chin thoughtfully. 'Keep at it. All is well for now, but we can't let anything—or anyone get past us. Understood?' he commanded, his eyes scanning the church.

The officers acknowledged their senior officer's orders and moved off to continue with their duties.

'Morning, Reverend Morton,' Peter said as the vicar turned from the altar, looking surprised as a Police Labrador's tail vanished into his vestry.

'Detective Inspector,' the reverend responded, a note of surprise in his voice. 'Quite the stir you've brought to our tranquil sanctuary. At least it usually is.'

'Please accept my apologies for the intrusion, Reverend,' Peter responded, scratching his head. 'But we can't leave anything to chance, not with Lister's knack for trouble.'

The vicar nodded, a chuckle despite the situation. 'Well, I suppose if there's any place to seek hidden sins, it's here. Though I dare say this isn't quite what I had in mind.'

Before Peter could reply, Sergeant Dawes approached, his boots echoing on the ancient flagstones. 'Sir, the interior's all clear.'

'Excellent work, Sergeant. Now, let's be thorough with the grounds, but mind the gravestones, eh? Sacred land and all that.'

'Of course, sir,' the sergeant affirmed, while casting a respectful glance towards the vicar.

As the bustle of police activity receded, Peter stood alongside Reverend Morton. Both men recognised the profound stillness that had reclaimed the church. Stained glass scenes bathed them in a kaleidoscope of colours, and the heady scent of lilies mingled with beeswax and old wood.

'Beautiful, isn't it?' the vicar murmured, his gaze lifting

to the timber vaulted ceiling. 'Even after all these years, it never ceases to amaze me.'

'Indeed, Reverend.' Peter sighed, feeling his shoulders ease off. 'Today, of all days, it needs to be a sanctuary in more ways than one.'

———

Saturday, 6th September: 7.40 am

ANT SPEARED a piece of perfectly crisped bacon with his fork. Morning sunlight streamed through the tall bay window of Stanton Hall's dining room. The effect painted golden stripes across the antique table. The Earl and Countess Stanton, his parents, sat across from him. They looked proud and nervous, like everyone else except the groom.

'Peter's done it,' Ant announced, his voice a low rumble of gratitude amid the clinking of China. 'Fitch just rang. They've got Lister in custody.'

Relief washed over his parents as they exchanged glances, a silent conversation passing between. The countess leaned forward, her silver-white hair catching the sunlight in a shimmering halo around her head. 'Oh, thank goodness. It's a weight off our minds, isn't it, dear?' she said, her voice soft but filled with genuine relief.

The Earl nodded, a small smile playing on his lips as he reached out to pat his wife's hand. 'Indeed, my darling. Peter always comes through when it matters most,' he remarked, his gaze turning to Ant with pride shining in his eyes. 'You've done well to bring him into the fold, son. Men like that are worth their weight in gold.'

Ant's chest swelled with pride at his parents' words, a

sense of accomplishment warming him from within. 'Peter's been invaluable in all this,' he agreed, spearing another piece of bacon thoughtfully.

'Let's hope that's the last of the drama for today,' the countess declared, her eyes sparkling and edged with humour and determination.

———

Saturday, 6th September: 7.40 am

JENNIFER'S HAIR salon buzzed with the excitement usually reserved for royal affairs. Lyn, seated before a mirror framed with bulbs, watched as Jennifer, the salon owner, wielded her scissors like an artist with a brush.

Jennifer's movements were swift and assured, her reflection in the mirror a blur of focused energy. Lyn marvelled at her skill, feeling a sense of relaxation wash over her as the strands of her hair fell to the floor like golden confetti.

Yet the thought of Lister dragged her thoughts on the situation. As the soft chatter of the salon buzzed around her.

'Looking lovely as always, Lyn,' Jennifer complimented with a smile, holding up a mirror for Lyn to inspect her freshly styled hair.

Lyn studied her reflection, a smile playing on her lips. 'Thank you, Jennifer. You've worked your magic once again.'

'Can't wait to hear about the honeymoon,' Jennifer said, snipping away. Meanwhile Lyn's maid of honour, Tina, sat in an adjacent styling chair, armed with a schedule and a determined look.

'First things first,' Tina interjected, glancing at the printed itinerary. 'We need to keep Fitch on track—'

Lyn's mobile interrupted her, its cheerful ringtone cutting through the hum of hairdryers and chatter. She answered, her heart skipping a beat as Fitch's voice confirmed what she had hoped to hear.

'Lister's behind bars,' Lyn announced.

Overwhelmed by a surge of relief, Lyn's worries melted away, leaving her light enough to float right out of the stylist's chair. She shared the news with the room, and a collective cheer erupted from the congregation of local women.

'Finally, some peace of mind,' Lyn beamed, exchanging a triumphant glance with Tina. 'Now, let's make sure this wedding goes off without a hitch!'

'Or a snip!' Jennifer quipped, deftly shaping the final curls around Lyn's shoulders. They laughed; the joyous sound mingling with the redolence of hairspray and the promise of a perfect day ahead.

————

Saturday, 6th September: 7.45 am

PETER EASED his police car off the tarmac and onto a narrow grass track. The tyres crunched softly against the dew-drenched earth. He pulled to a stop and turned off the engine, the sudden silence enveloping him like a soft blanket. With a contented sigh, he stepped out of the vehicle and leaned back against the weathered wood of an old field gate, its timbers smooth from years of handling.

The Norfolk countryside stretched before him, a patchwork quilt of emerald green fields and hedgerows. The morning sun cast long shadows across the gently undulating land. Two chestnut horses graze nearby, their tails flicking lazily, the very picture of rural serenity.

On noticing Peter's presence, they ambled over—a pair of equine aristocrats gracing a commoner with their attention. He greeted them with a smile, his hand extended in silent offering. They nuzzled his palm, warm breath tickling his skin as he stroked their sleek necks. Their manes rippled with each gentle brush, the simple act grounding him further in the moment.

'Morning, you two,' Peter murmured affectionately, reaching into his jacket pocket. The crinkle of the mint packet acted like a siren call. The horses' ears pricked up in eager anticipation. He unwrapped a couple of sweets and laid them flat on his open hand. The horses lipped at the mints with enthusiasm, their velvety muzzles brushing against his skin.

A chuckle escaped Peter as he watched them enjoy their treat. The tension that had knotted his shoulders now unravelled. Control—a feeling as elusive as mist over the past chaotic days—finally settled comfortably within him. 'Today was going to be a good day,' he thought to himself.

The pastoral idyll lulled him into a brief respite, the worries about Lister and his ominous plans fading into the background. But like a cloud passing over the sun, the peace was transient. His mobile buzzed against his thigh, the ringtone slicing through the hush of the countryside.

'Detective Inspector Riley,' he answered, the confidence in his voice belied by the tightening in his gut.

'Sir, we've got a situation,' came the clipped voice of a junior officer. 'North Walsham, picked up a man. Overheard boasting in a pub about something big planned for today in Stanton Parva—something that'll make him famous. The local lot are transporting him to Stanton Parva as we speak, sir.'

Peter's heart sank. 'So much for control', he thought as he thanked the officer and hung up. The vast sky suddenly felt oppressive, the horizon too far away. He looked back at the horses, their innocent eyes offering no counsel. Peter wondered whether Lister's threat was about to materialise.

Chapter Ten

TRUTH OR DELUSION?

Saturday, 6th September 8.55 am

PETER LISTENED CALMLY to the constable's report as the office clock in the police station ticked towards nine. Constable Evans, a man whose ears seem perpetually pink from the brisk Norfolk air, shuffled from one foot to the other before clearing his throat.

'OK, sir,' he began, looking nervously at Peter. 'We picked up a Mr. Timothy Rudge, 34 years of age. Looks rough around the edges. Says he's got something planned for Stanton Parva. That'll put him in the history books.'

Peter raised an eyebrow but said nothing, giving the constable room to elaborate.

'Claims he's going to do something today—something big,' Evans continued, scratching his head. 'He's been all chatter since we collected him, but whether there's truth in his words or it's all just bluster, well, I don't know, sir.'

'Thank you, Evans. I'll take it from here,' Peter replied,

his voice calm and measured. He stood and made for the interview room, where Rudge awaited.

The space was stark, save for the table and chairs bolted to the floor. The man sitting across from Peter matched the constable's description: a bit dishevelled, with a nervous energy about him.

'Detective! You heard about my grand plan, I presume?' Rudge exclaimed, his eyes glinting with what could either be excitement or madness.

'Let's start with your intentions, Mr. Rudge,' Peter coaxed, taking a seat opposite him. 'Tell me, what exactly do you have planned for Stanton Parva?'

Rudge leaned forward conspiratorially. 'It's not every day you get to shake up a sleepy village like this one, right? I'm gonna be famous, Detective. Infamous, more like.' His laugh was a little too loud, echoing off the painted walls of the small room.

'Infamy comes at a cost,' Peter remarked, his tone still even as he watched Rudge for any telltale signs of deception or delusion. 'Why Stanton Parva, though? Do you have any connections here?'

'Nah, no connections. But it's the perfect place, isn't it? All those posh people gathering for the wedding of the century,' Rudge said, tapping the side of his nose. 'You'll see. I'll make headlines.'

Peter nods, making mental notes while avoiding any direct mention of Lister. He couldn't risk leading the witness, especially if Rudge's tale had any truth to it. Yet, if there's a thread linking this man to the mastermind behind the threats to Ant and Lyn's wedding, Peter needed to find it without tipping his hand.

'Tell me about your past, Mr. Rudge. Have you done

anything like this before?' Peter asked, probing deeper without revealing his own hand.

'Nothing this grand, Detective. But I've always been a man of ambition,' Rudge boasted, his chest puffing out. 'You might say I've been preparing for this my whole life.'

'Preparation is key,' Peter murmured, his mind racing. Was Rudge simply a pawn in Lister's game, or was he an independent agent acting on his own misguided desire for recognition?

The question hung in the air, unanswered. Peter knew precious time was passing; he couldn't let Rudge walk free for now, yet he had no solid grounds to keep him detained. As the minutes slipped by, the pressure mounted to unravel the truth from the tapestry of lies—or perhaps just delusions—that Rudge wove.

'Stay put, Mr. Rudge. We're not done yet,' Peter said, standing up. Rudge smirked, enjoying the attention.

'Take your time, Detective. I'm not going anywhere,' Rudge replied, his voice oozing a confidence that sent a chill down Peter's spine.

As Peter exited the room, he knew one thing for certain: he had to tread carefully. The success of a certain wedding could depend on his next move.

'Keep thinking you're the star of the show,' Peter muttered under as he strode purposefully down the corridor toward his office. The click of his shoes on the linoleum punctuated each step like a metronome, keeping time with his racing thoughts.

Once secluded behind the privacy of his desk, Peter picked up the telephone receiver and dialled the North Walsham station. He asked to speak with the arresting officer.

'Constable Roberts speaking,' a voice responded after a moment, tinny through the speaker.

'Detective Inspector Riley here, from Stanton Parva,' he said succinctly. 'I'm looking into the bloke you sent over—Rudge. What's his story?'

'Rudge? Ah, yes. Known for spinning tales taller than the church steeple. Got caught nicking garden gnomes last spring, if you can believe it.'

'Sounds like quite the character,' Peter replied, his mouth curling in amusement. 'Anything else I should know?'

'Only that he seemed oddly well-versed in Lord Stanton's wedding details. He bragged about making a name for himself,' constable Evans adds, a note of caution creeping into his voice.

'Thank you, constable. That's fleshed the fella out a bit for me. I owe you one.' Peter hung up, drumming his fingers on the icy surface of the desk.

Letting Rudge stew might shake loose some truth, or at least give him time to sort fact from fiction. He glanced at the clock; the minutes seem to tick by. 'One hour,' he decided, standing again. 'Then we'll see what our Mr. Rudge is really about.'

Saturday, 6th September 10.00 am

THE OLD SCHOOLHOUSE was alive with the effervescent energy that only a wedding morning can conjure. Friends and family gathered downstairs, creating an exciting atmosphere with their laughter and voices.

Upstairs, Lyn stood in her room, the sunlight pouring

through the window, bathing her in a warm glow. Her eyes sparkled with excitement as she gazed at the wedding dress laid out on her bed—the lace, the silk, a dream soon to become reality.

'Isn't it just perfect?' Tina exclaims, her hands flitting about her own styled hair as if trying to contain her glee.

'More perfect than I imagined,' Lyn breathed, reaching a hand to trace the delicate embroidery. The dress whispered secrets of joy and tomorrow's memories.

Downstairs, the essence of freshly ground coffee permeated every corner as the percolator gurgled and hissed its steamy siren song.

Amid the household scene, undercover officers seamlessly merged with the surroundings. They were watchful guardians, ensuring nothing disturbed the harmony of Lyn's special day.

'In a few hours...' Tina trails off, her words hanging like a suspended chord, full of possibility.

Lyn nodded, her heart swelling with a cocktail of nerves and elation. The reflection in the mirror showed a woman ready to embrace a new chapter. Her blond hair framed her face like a halo, her happiness shining through the softness of her features.

'Let's make sure those hours count,' Lyn said, her voice steady, her resolve clear. She was not one to be intimidated, not today, never.

Back downstairs, a precarious truce held as Lyn's divorced parents navigated their daughter's wedding day. Her father, a stoic figure with eyes that hid years of regret with an amiable smile, had commandeered the study. He sat, posture impeccable, occasionally glancing towards the door as if expecting conflict to waltz through at any moment.

Across the hall, her mother—a woman whose sharp mind was matched only by the cut of her tailored dress, settled in the conservatory. She gazed out onto the garden, the vibrant blossoms belying the tension that clung like the morning dew. A solitary cup of tea cooled on the table beside her, untouched, its steam curling upward and vanishing into nothingness.

Lyn had laid down the law: 'You will behave, or else.'

A chaperone tasked with a tough diplomatic mission shadowed each parent. With subtle signals and meaningful looks, Tina directed the peacekeepers to do their job without drawing attention.

'Remember,' Tina whispered, 'keep them apart, keep them happy, and for heaven's sake, keep them quiet.'

The chaperones nodded. They stood ready to intercept any stray comment or accidental encounter that might set off familial fireworks.

Saturday, 6th September 10.00 am

STANTON HALL STOOD regal amidst the Norfolk landscape, its grandeur undiminished by time. Inside, the library offered sanctuary to Ant, who lounged in a deep armchair, a history book resting open on his lap. The only sound in the room was the rhythmic ticking of the grandfather clock that had been there for centuries. Its pendulum swung back and forth, a hypnotic metronome counting down the hours to matrimony.

Ant glanced at the magnificent timepiece, his gaze lingering on the ornate hands as they counted down the time towards half-past two. The serenity of the grounds belied the flurry of activity within the Great Hall. Staff and hired help moved with purpose, an orchestrated chaos invisible to the casual observer.

David, the butler, surveyed his domain with the calm eye of a seasoned general. His movements precise, each adjustment of cutlery a silent command. He straightened a fork here, aligned a wine glass there—every action measured, every detail critical to the impending celebration.

'Everything must be perfect,' he murmured to himself, though his expression betrayed no hint of doubt. Under his watchful management, the hall became transformed into a stage set for joy, awaiting the arrival of the day's stars.

Saturday, 6th September 10.00 am

REVEREND MORTON WAS busy inside the village church, guiding his volunteers with passion and enthusiasm. 'Mind the lilies on the altar,' he chirped, his voice echoing through the hallowed nave like the song of a pious sparrow.

The church warden, a sturdy pillar of the parish, took meticulous care in positioning the place cards. Each bore a name, as testament to the community's tightly knit fabric, and august visitors for the day. The organist perched high up played delightful music, filling the space with a cascade of notes that danced among the stone arches.

A lone constable wearing the mantle of vigilance, with a sense of muted pride, made his rounds. His footsteps were soft against the ancient floor, a silent promise to safeguard the joyous day ahead.

Saturday, 6th September 10.30 am

AT GUNTON PARK STATION, Peter stood amidst a scene plucked from a bygone era. The platform was quiet in the morning sun, except for the occasional rustling of wildlife. It might be easy to imagine the shrill whistle and billowing steam of a locomotive from days past.

'Did he meet anyone?' Peter asked, his voice cutting through the pastoral stillness. The stationmaster, a man whose features were as much a part of the station as the worn wooden benches, shook his head. He repeated the information to Peter, his memory clear despite the mundane nature of their previous conversation.

'Blue jacket, casual trousers,' the stationmaster recollected, scratching at the stubble on his chin. 'Had a backpack, he did.'

Peter's mind grapples with the image—now familiar—but something was missing. 'And the suitcase?' he prodded gently, knowing the importance of what wasn't said.

'Suitcase?' The stationmaster's brow deepened like a ploughed field. 'No, no suitcase that I saw.'

Alarm bells tolled in Peter's head, not unlike the Sunday peal that calls the faithful to worship. The implications spread before him; a sinister shadow crept across the bucolic landscape.

'Are you certain?' Peter insisted, urgency sharpening his tone.

'Sure as the 9:15 is always late on a Thursday,' the stationmaster replied with unwavering conviction.

At that moment, Peter understood; the game had changed. A suitcase unaccounted for—a vessel for unknown dangers—had vanished into the Norfolk countryside. With a wedding set to be the talk of the region, every second became precious, every decision critical.

———

Saturday, 6th September 11.15 am

PETER, with the urgency of a summer storm, burst through the doors of Stanton Parva's police station, his mind churning like the gears of an old car.

'Lister,' he demanded, his voice a controlled calm that belayed the tempest within. 'Bring him to Interview Room Two.'

Constables scurry about, their movements echoing Peter's internal rush. As the man from North Walsham sat in the adjacent room, inventing grandiose fictions, Peter prepared for a duel of wits with a far more cunning opponent.

Lister arrived, the click-clack of his handcuffs punctuating each step. He smirked as he sat opposite Peter, the expression cutting across his face—unnatural and alarming.

'Found your little surprise yet, Peter?' Lister teased, his voice dripping with a confidence that unsettled his opponent.

Peter's pulse quickened, but his face remained an unreadable mask, a poker face perfected dealing with the likes of Lister. He leaned back in his chair, adopting an air of nonchalance.

'Surprises are for birthdays, Ian. And you're not the party type, are you?' Peter retorted, parrying the verbal thrust with ease.

Peter nonchalantly referred to someone being overly chatty about the upcoming events.

Lister's eyes remained as still as the surface of a millpond. Peter recognised the man was as much a mentor as an adversary, having taught Peter the very skills he's now used against him.

'Talkative people can create messy situations, right, Ian?' Peter watched every expression, every twitch for a sign of recognition or alarm.

But Lister was a fortress, a stronghold of secrets, giving nothing away. His smirk merely deepened, etching lines of arrogance into his face as if the sculptor of his own dubious legend.

Peter internally nodded to himself, acknowledging the level of game he'd engaged in. To reveal too much would be to hand Lister the keys to the kingdom; to say too little would be to let the villain believe he had the upper hand. It was a high-wire act above a field of nettles, and Peter balanced with the skill of a seasoned acrobat.

'Your move, Lister,' Peter thought, but wisely kept the words unspoken. The dance of detectives and deviants continued, one beat away from a crescendo.

Peter stood, a statue of composure, but inside the storm raged. With every tick of the clock on the station wall, memories flashed like lightning—cases unsolved. Criminals that slipped through his fingers turned clumsy with doubt. The echo of Lister's smirk seemed to bounce off the walls, taunting him. Peter knew what was at stake; not just his reputation, but lives hanging in the balance.

He recalled Phyllis once comparing her failed Victoria sponge to the Leaning Tower of Pisa - a disaster, yet still standing. He looked for that resilience now.

Peter rose and knocked on the door of the interview room. 'Take this man back to his cell. Earlier communication orders remain in force.'

Now alone, he paced back and forth in the narrow confines of his office, the worn carpet fibres a testament to countless such deliberations. His mind rehearsed each move, each countermove. Lister's words, 'Have you found my little surprise?' lingered. Peter shook his head as if to dispel an annoying fly; Lister's games were growing tiresome.

'Time to flip the script,' Peter decided, his resolve hardening. He imagined himself a knight in a game of chess, moving unpredictably, throwing Lister's strategy into disarray. Every failure had been a lesson wrapped in the guise of defeat, and he wouldn't let it happen again.

'Constable,' Peter called out, summoning the young officer waiting outside. 'A cup of tea if you'd be so kind. One sugar, no milk.' Even amid mental warfare, there was always time for tea.

'Right away, sir,' the constable answered, eager to please. Peter watched him go, the click of the door closing a signal for the last act.

Outside, the sun rose higher as mid-morning arrived. Peter's steely eyes watched as villagers busied themselves with the daily routine. Today, he spotted they moved with more of a spring in their step at the joyous day to come. At least that's what he wanted to believe.

Just then, the constable returned with a steaming mug of tea, placing it on Peter's desk with a soft clink that punctuated the silence. Peter offered a thankful nod, his hand closing around the warm mug as he sipped and allowed himself a moment of respite. Yet behind those thoughtful sips, his mind raced, piecing together fragments like a jigsaw puzzle missing its ultimate piece.

Suddenly, the phone rang—a piercing trill that sliced through the quiet with urgency. Peter's hand halted mid-air, tea forgotten. He set down the mug with careful precision and reached for the receiver. His grip is firm, betraying none of the tension that coiled within him. 'Detective Inspector Peter Riley,' he answered, his voice strong despite his quickening pulse.

As he listened to the voice on the other end—a voice laced with hesitant trepidation. The news was unexpected; an uninvited twist in an already tangled mystery. Slowly placing the receiver back on its cradle, Peter stood and straightened his jacket with a sharp tug.

Somewhere, just beyond sight, through hushed reeds and over gentle fields, lay Dipping Lane Forge, a place he hadn't heard of before. Another piece of the puzzle waited to leap forth from shadow to light. Could this be the luck that had evaded him these past days? Or would it waste precious time he didn't have? Peter had no choice; he had to take a chance.

Chapter Eleven

A SUITED GENTLEMAN

Saturday, 11.50 am

DETECTIVE INSPECTOR PETER RILEY eased his police car onto a grass verge alongside Dipping Lane Forge; the venerable structure all but swallowed by nature's embrace. The lane itself—a mere whisper of a road—tunnelled through an overgrowth of elm and willow, their leaves interlocking above to form a verdant canopy. Despite the late summer warmth, here beneath this arboreal vault, the air clung with a cool dampness that seemed to defy of the season.

Before him, nestled within the clutch of greenery, stood the forge. Its walls cloaked in ivy. Shadows gathered greedily at its arched entrance. A black car, as nondescript as a rainy English day, languished just beyond the entrance, its presence an enigma. Who did it belong to? Peter had no clue, but harboured a quiet hope, a flicker in the fog of uncertainty. 'Let this be the lead that unravels Lister's nefarious web,' Peter thought.

Peter switched the engine off, half expecting to glimpse

his mysterious contact from within the safety of his vehicle. However, the single-story edifice played its cards close to the chest, revealing nothing. Sighing, Peter stepped out into the muted light, his shoes crunching softly on the stoney soil as he approached the mouth of the forge.

He paused at the entrance, peering into the gloom where daylight fought to penetrate. Inside, the forge's ancient heartbeat no more; scattered tools lay silent, their rusted edges speaking of a time when fire danced and metal sang under the hand of a master craftsman. Peter ventured deeper, each step stirring echoes in the semi-darkness.

As he cautiously navigated the dimly lit interior, Detective Inspector Peter Riley's eyes scanned the abandoned forge for any signs of life or recent activity. The air was heavy with the aroma of old smoke and charred wood, invoking a sense of nostalgia for a bygone era when the forge was alive with the clanging of hammers and the hiss of molten metal.

Just as Peter's hand brushed against a dusty workbench cluttered with half-finished projects, a faint noise caught his attention. It was a soft rustling sound, as if someone were trying to move without being noticed.

Heart thumping, Peter crept towards the source of the noise—a shadowy alcove obscured by tattered curtains. With bated breath, he pulled the fabric aside to reveal a figure perched on an old crate.

'Detective Inspector Riley, thank you for coming,' came a voice, smooth as polished silver, slicing through the quiet. It wasn't menacing, but the sort one might hear inquiring about the quality of a sponge cake at a local fete. The venue fit neither the disused forge, nor the clandestine nature of their meeting, yet here they were, and with it, perhaps, the break Peter had been seeking.

Peter's gaze settled on the figure seated amidst the shadows. The man's striped suit was a splash of civilisation against the rustic backdrop, his posture relaxed yet dignified as he perched on a timeworn wooden box. An umbrella, the very model of British propriety, stood vigil beside him, propped neatly against the gnarled wall. The stranger's shoes, in contrast to the detritus-strewn floor, gleamed with an almost obsessive polish.

'Thank you for the call,' Peter offered, his tone mirroring the quiet of their surroundings. Despite the peculiarity of their meeting place and the secrets it surely held, a wave of inexplicable calm washed over him. They lingered in a silent appraisal, two statues carved from different eras, momentarily frozen in time.

'Seems you've got one up on me,' Peter finally broke the stillness, a grin inching across his face. 'You know who I am, but I'm at a loss.'

'Ah, my apologies,' The gentleman remarked as he unfolded himself from his makeshift seat, standing tall and lean before Peter. 'I'm Siegfried Schultze. A slip of etiquette on my part.'

'Your English is impeccable,' Peter observed, unable to resist the compliment.

'Thank you kindly,' Siegfried replied, his smile warming the cool air. 'My father hailed from Germany, but I'm Chipping Norton born and bred. As British as Bangers and Mash, despite the name.'

'Chipping Norton, you say?' Peter echoed, amusement lacing his voice. 'Well, Mr Schultze, I must admit you have a knack for the dramatic. Quite the scenic spot you've chosen for our little chat.' His eyes twinkled with mirth as he gestured around the dim forge.

Siegfried chuckled, a deep, melodic sound that filled the

space between them. 'A touch of theatrics hurt no one, Detective Inspector. Besides, a bit of mystery adds spice to life, wouldn't you agree?'

Peter's mouth tilted upward as the light-hearted quip diffused the last remnants of tension. There was an ease to Siegfried's manner that felt decidedly out of step with the cryptic nature of their encounter—a pleasant incongruity that Peter couldn't help but appreciate.

'Curiosity may have killed the cat, Mr. Schultze, but I'm not feline—just a man wondering why he's in an old forge with a stranger,' Peter quipped with restrained levity as he watched Siegfried's composed demeanour. 'What's all this about?'

'Ah, Detective Inspector Riley, you see, we both have an interest in a certain ex-commander, Lister,' Siegfried began, his voice concealing unspoken secrets. 'He turned up in Stanton Parva, and I bear partial responsibility for that.'

Peter's heart kicked against his chest like a trapped bird. Could Siegfried be another piece in Lister's devious game, setting the stage for some grand escape? He stole himself, ready to tackle whatever came next.

'Let's cut to the chase, Mr Schultze. Are you part of Lister's machinations?' Peter's eyes narrowed, scrutinising the other man for any telltale sign of deceit.

'Detective, I assure you, you've misconstrued my words.' Siegfried held up a hand, pausing Peter's burgeoning tirade. 'I represent a certain department with interests... beyond the local constabulary's usual purview.'

'And this 'department' needed Lister out of prison because...?' Peter prompted, disbelief etching his features.

'His expertise was required for... a task of some important to His Majesty's government,' Siegfried replied calmly. 'We orchestrated his escape without the knowledge of the prison governor. Lister himself is unaware of the full picture and the part we've allotted to him. He has a part to play and he must act it out.'

'Right, and next you'll tell me the Queen knits tea cosies,' Peter deadpanned, his astonishment giving way to suspicion. He envisioned Lyn and Ant on this of all days. If Siegfried was playing games, they could all pay the price.

Unmoved by Siegfried's earnest words, Peter's gaze remained steely as he contemplated the man before him. The implications of Lister's escape reached far beyond the quaint locality. The man threatened to unravel the fabric of trust that bound its residents together. His presence also threatened the lives of his two closest friends.

'I won't stand idly by while you sow chaos in our community, Mr Schultze,' Peter declared, his voice firm. 'If you have any regard for the people of Stanton Parva, you'll cooperate with me and tell me everything you know about Lister.'

Siegfried met Peter's steely gaze with a mixture of resignation and respect. Though their encounter had begun in shadows and half-truths, a glimmer of understanding now flickered between them.

'Believe what you will, but my regret about Lyn Blackthorn, and Lord Anthony, is genuine,' Siegfried continued, earnestness creeping into his tone. 'I'll apologise in person on completion of my task.'

'Completion? How?' Peter asked, the word 'apology' hanging in the air like a spectre. 'Lister's in custody, sure, but there's a suitcase out there. Something tells me it's not packed for a holiday.'

'Indeed, Lister has gone rogue. He shouldn't be anywhere near your patch,' Siegfried conceded, a shadow crossing his sharp features. 'The extent of his hatred towards Ms Blackthorn and Lord Anthony came as a surprise. My department had only its own intentions in mind when we facilitated his... departure from residing at His Majesty's pleasure.'

Peter's mind raced, a turbulent storm of thoughts swirled within him.

'Siegfried, you can't expect us to believe that Lister's sudden allegiance to your department's cause is genuine,' Peter asserted, a sharp edge to his voice betraying his growing unease. 'He's a master manipulator, and whatever he's planning now puts everyone in Stanton Parva at risk.'

Siegfried regarded Peter with a solemn expression, his gaze unwavering as he acknowledged the severity of their predicament. 'I understand your apprehension, Detective Inspector. Lister's actions have veered wildly from the course we set him. In doing so, he's posing a threat we must now neutralise.'

Siegfried's words hung heavily in the air, casting a shadow over their conversation. Peter knew that time was of the essence.

'Rogue' wasn't a word Peter liked, especially when paired with 'Lister.' He felt the prickle of unease as if nettles had brushed against his skin. 'I know he had a suitcase with him when he arrived. Until I find it, my officers remain on high alert.'

'Quite the predicament,' Siegfried murmured, the slightest hint of empathy peeking through his formal facade. 'But, Detective Inspector, I am here to assist you in that matter.'

Peter nodded, though the promise offered little comfort. The countryside offered tranquillity, but beneath its serene façade, danger lurked, nestled among the hedgerows, and haunting the quiet lanes. For now, he had to trust the enigmatic stranger and hope that the whispers of wildlife carried no ill tidings.

Peter's gaze narrowed as Siegfried unfolded, a tale more twisted than the ivy clinging to the forge walls. 'So you see,' Siegfried continued. 'I may be of some help.'

'Go on,' Peter prompted, though the sceptic in him braced for tough news.

'Since Lister's departure from our... safe house, we've kept a watchful eye on him.' Siegfried detailed Lister's wanderings with the precision of an owl tracking its prey. 'The church, the dilapidated dwelling where the old man gained clothing, and one other location — elusive to you thus far.'

Peter's mind raced to connect the dots. However, Siegfried cut through his thoughts with a proposition that carried the chill of the damp forge. 'We need Lister to make another exit, Detective.'

'Escape? Again?' Peter exploded, his words ricocheting off cold stone like misguided bullets. 'Have you considered the risk to Anthony Stanton and Lyn Blackthorn? To all of Stanton Parva?'

'Risks we can manage,' Siegfried responded, his tone as smooth as the polished shoes on his feet. He betrayed no hint of jest. 'They need not know a thing.'

Lying to them felt like swallowing a wasp. Yet hadn't Peter been prepared to do just that recently? His principles tangled like falling into a hedge of brambles.

'What's my end of the bargain?' Peter grumbled, feeling like he's negotiating with a fox for the safety of the hens.

'Two things: the exact lair where Lister has burrowed himself away, and a name.' Siegfried's offer hung in the air, tantalising, tantalising yet terrifying.

'A name?' Peter echoed, confusion tormenting his thoughts.

'I know Lister's hinted he's not a lone wolf in this countryside caper,' Siegfried continued. 'And the identity of his little helper will shock you.'

Time seemed to tick louder in Peter's ear as he glanced at his mobile, aware that each second passing was a decision delayed. 'Who?' he pressed, not missing the irony that this could well be the twist in his own village mystery novel.

Siegfried held the pause like a conductor before the last note of a symphony. 'Jemma Cole.'

'Jemma Cole?' Peter tasted the name like a dubious pie filling. Then it clicked—the persistent reporter who had tangled herself in the Amber Burton case like yarn in a kitten's paws. 'She got close to Lister's son, Thomas, didn't she?'

'Indeed,' Siegfried confirmed with a nod, his expression unreadable as a sphinx.

Wry humour danced at the edges of Peter's conscience despite the situation. Mystery, intrigue, and now an unexpected ally of a newspaper hawk.

'Let me guess, she's penning a new chapter in her career by abetting?' Peter asked, though he wasn't sure if he wanted to hear the answer.

Siegfried's revelation caused a seismic shift in his understanding of the case. 'But Thomas is in prison—doing a long stretch for Spinner's murder,' he protested, his voice barely more than a whisper in the hush of the old forge.

'Quite so,' Siegfried agreed, his tone measured and even. 'And while Jemma Cole's correspondence with young Mr. Lister has waned. But her past usefulness to him kindled an idea to our friend currently enjoying Her Majesty's hospitality in one of your cells.' He paused, allowing the implications to bloom like a dark rose in Peter's mind. 'Lister leveraged that old connection. Convinced her to find him somewhere safe to hide out. She gave him a key to her family's holiday home.'

'Blackmail,' Peter hissed, the word tasting bitter on his tongue.

'An effective motivator,' Siegfried replied, offering a small piece of paper. 'The address...and her mobile number. Might be worth a chat, don't you think?'

Peter's heart raced as he stared at the piece of paper in Siegfried's outstretched hand. The address and mobile number burned into his mind, a lifeline in the tangled web of deception and danger that surrounded Stanton Parva. With a nod of gratitude, Peter pocketed the vital information, steeling himself for the task ahead.

'Siegfried, you're asking me to trust you,' Peter began, his voice laced with a newfound determination. 'And I will, for now. But know this-if anything happens to Anthony, Lyn, or anyone in the village because of your plan, there will be consequences.'

Siegfried met Peter's gaze with a steely resolve that matched the detective's own. 'Understood, Detective Inspector,' he replied evenly. 'Our interests may align for now, I assure you. Stanton Parva is paramount to me, too.'

With an unspoken understanding passing between them, Peter turned to leave the forge

'And what am I to do for the information?'.

'You have already delivered it,' Siegfried admitted with an infuriating nonchalance. 'By now, Lister will be a free man again. Don't worry, my people have eyes on him. He's oblivious to this. We are, and will remain, close enough to blow on the nape of his neck if we need to.'

'Marvellous,' Peter grumbled, sarcasm dripping from

each syllable. He wanted to trust this immaculate stranger, but in the pit of his stomach, there was a churn of doubt. The sort that came with what scant knowledge he had of government intelligence services.

'So, I have to deal with the fallout, and embarrassment of explaining how I allowed an escaped prisoner, eh, to escape again? The local press will have a field day, and that's without what my superiors will have in store for me. Did you think about any of that?'

'Don't worry about any of that. My department will ensure the press is told one thing, and your superior's, the truth…as far as we can do so without jeopardising national security.'

Peter shook his head. 'The world has gone nuts. Anyway, what I don't get why you haven't spirited him away, so he can do whatever it was you sprung him from jail for? Why did you let him go, given the risk to Athony Stanton and Lyn Blackthorn?' Peter said, his gaze looked as confused as his voice sounded.'

'Detective Inspector Riley,' Siegfried intoned solemnly, 'This is a nasty business. However, let me assure you your friends will come to no harm. If all goes well, they won't even be aware of anything out of the ordinary happening today… apart from their wedding, of course.' The stranger's disarming smile emerged from his earlier serious tone.

'That still doesn't answer my question.'

'It's all I can say for now, I'm afraid. That said, I promise to tell you the reason before the day is out.'

'That's reassuring, I suppose,' Peter muttered, though his confidence had taken a hard knock. With additional officers keeping watch unseen around the quaint village, he had little choice but to play along with the game. What a tale he'd have for Ant and Lyn when all this was over.

'Rogues and reporters,' he sighed, 'All hidden among the hedgerows.' There was a brief pause as he glanced out at the tree canopy sheltering them from the sun. A leach storm-petrel chortled, blissfully unaware of human follies.

'Norfolk's wildlife,' Peter quipped, trying to grasp at the lighter side of life as he always did, 'Another creature for the local birdwatchers to tick off their list.'

'Rare sighting indeed,' Siegfried replied, the ghost of a smile fleeting across his features before vanishing like mist over the Broads.

Peter stepped back into his police car, readying himself to confront the next twist in Stanton Parva's serpentine story.

––––––––

Saturday, 6th September 12.40 am

THE DETECTIVE'S mind raced as the car devoured the distance to the holiday cottage, a quaint stone structure with an obedient thatch that seemed to bow under the weight of its own rustic charm. As he pulled up, he felt a pinch of relief at the sight of the cottage standing back from the road —a silent guardian of secrets yet untold. The frontage was plain and unassuming, like a poker-faced confidant in a game of cat-and-mouse.

He walked up the drive, his footsteps hesitant, half-expecting a trap or an ambush. The Norfolk air wrapped around him, thick with the scent of cut grass and a faint undertone of manure—a reminder of the landscape's unspoiled innocence that had been so rudely disrupted by intrigue. With a glance at his mobile. For once, he felt gratitude for the non-existent signal.

As Jemma opened the door, their expressions mirrored each other—twin portraits of shock. Peter's gaze was sharp, piercing; hers wide-eyed, a fawn caught in the glare of unsolicited attention.

'Jemma Cole,' Peter began, not bothering with pleasantries, 'I know all about your contact with Lister.' His voice had the edge of a well-honed blade, one he was reluctant to sheathe despite the situation.

She ushered him into the heart of the cottage, a small, and unpretentious space, yet now harboured a viper's egg. Jemma cried floods of tears. Peter watched her with the scepticism of a seasoned detective who'd seen too many tears used as smokescreens. Despite himself, he softened after enduring the relentless cascade of her sobs.

'I think I understand a little of what's been going on, but don't have the time for you to explain. That time will come soon. For now, please show me the suitcase,' he asked, his voice firm but kind.

He followed the sobbing woman up the narrow stairs and into a small, comfortably decorated bedroom. The object sat on the bed like a relic of bygone travels, its corners bruised with age and escapades. Half-torn labels told a tale of travels to Istanbul and Quebec. Now it rested under the scrutiny of a British detective,

Peter approached with the caution. His fingers grazed the latches, and the snap of the lock plates breaking free echoed ominously through the stillness of the room.

'Here goes nothing,' he murmured and flipped the lid open.

A terrific bang shattered the quiet. Smoke billowed like a magician's grand finale gone awry.

The room fell silent. One down, two to go?

Chapter Twelve

BANG ON TIME

Saturday, 6th September 12.50 pm

THE WORLD CAME BACK into focus through a haze of dust and debris. Peter blinked rapidly, his vision clearing as the last remnants of the explosion's chaos settled around him like an unwelcome winter frost. The high-pitched ringing in his ears receded. Now the more familiar sounds of rural Norfolk sounded out: distant crows arguing over territory and the rustle of leaves in the gentle breeze.

He pushed himself up from the ground, a wince creasing his features as he felt the pull of strained muscles. He observed a minor burn on his arm and noticed his jacket had singed—a souvenir from the unexpected fire-works. Twisting to examine it, the skin was red and angry looking, but thankfully, it seemed superficial. He grimaced at the sting; the pain was sharp but not debilitating.

'Bit of a scorcher, that,' he muttered, trying to inject a bit of levity into the situation. There was something about the quaintness of the cottage that made even the thought of danger seem absurd, like a fox caught stealing scones from a picnic.

Peter's heart coursed with adrenaline, reminding him he was alive amid an unexpectedly explosive case. He flexed his fingers, feeling the burn stretch and pull, a tangible reminder of how close they'd come to a less fortunate outcome.

'Always fancied a bit of excitement,' he quipped to no one in particular. 'But I'll take a stolen cow over this, any day.'

Peter took a deep breath, smelling the odour of burnt wiring and leather. He shook his head, dislodging a rogue piece of ceiling plaster that had taken up residence in his hair during the commotion.

'Can't wait to explain this at the pub,' he mused. Peter imagined Phyllis' face alight with the prospect of such juicy gossip—no doubt it would become a tale of epic proportions by morning. He could almost hear her now, recounting how he'd leaped from the flames like a phoenix, or something equally embellished.

But there was no time for indulging in imaginary chatter. Duty called, and it was a call that Peter knew all too well. With a determined nod to the empty room, he set his jaw and prepared for the next phase of this most peculiar investigation.

His attention snapped to the stirring form of Jemma, who lay a few feet away amidst the debris. Her eyelids fluttered open, revealing dazed confusion as she tried to make sense of her surroundings. Dust motes danced in the surrounding light, like mischievous sprites playing in the aftermath of chaos.

'Jemma!' Peter called out, his voice steady despite the hammering of his heart. He scrambled over to her, his own injuries momentarily forgotten. He crouched beside the woman, his hands hovering protectively. 'Hey, are you alright?'

Her gaze wandered aimlessly before locking onto his. 'What... what happened?' she croaked; her voice was hoarse, as if the explosion had tried to steal it away.

'Explosion,' he confirmed with a nod to the disarray all around them, trying to keep his tone light despite the situation. 'We've had a bit of a ruckus, but we're both in one piece. More or less.'

She attempted a smile, her composure shaken by the blast. Peter helped her to sit up, checking her for injuries with an efficiency born of sorting out too many drunken punch-ups. When no obvious injuries presented themselves, he offered a reassuring grin. 'You'll have quite the tale for the book club next week.'

Jemma grimaced, brushing off her clothes as though she could simply wipe away the experience. 'I'd rather stick to Agatha Christie than live it, thank you very much.'

As she steadied herself, Peter's eyes fell on the remnants of their trouble: a battered leather case, its contents strewn about. Something didn't seem right, and that was saying something given its current state. With a furrowed brow, he inched closer, noticing a plastic wallet that appeared almost fused to the lining, as if it were hiding in plain sight.

'Lister,' he cursed.

Despite his burned fingers, he worked hard to remove the plastic from the fabric, then carefully pried the wallet free.

'Found something?' Jemma asked, her curiosity momentarily overpowering her disorientation.

'Perhaps,' Peter replied, concealing the triumphant twitch of his moustache. He held the wallet up to the light, examining it as one might a rare object unearthed at a local archaeological dig.

'Could be nothing. Then again, it might just be the breadcrumb we need.'

Jemma watched him with a mixture of apprehension and anticipation. She knew the wilds of Norfolk held secrets. The truth waiting for the keen eye of an unassuming village detective to bring them to light.

Peter slit the wallet open with his thumb, revealing a single sheet of thick, cream paper folded neatly within. The note, penned in an obnoxiously flamboyant scroll, read as if Lister himself were chuckling over his shoulder:

'Dear Peter,

Surprised? I must say, your persistence would be admirable if it weren't so predictably tedious. One might think you'd have learned by now that I'm always one step ahead. Like a fox eluding the hounds, I watch you scramble, ever so amusing.

I do hope you enjoyed the little fireworks display I left for you. As for my RSVP to dear Lyn's wedding, I won't be there in person. However, rest assured, you will feel my presence.

Your illustrious adversary,

Commander Lister (retired)

Peter's jaw tightened, the words stinging like nettles on bare skin. He could almost hear Lister's smug voice weaving through the script, each word dripping with derision. His hands trembled with a cocktail of anger and adrenaline; the audacity of the man was enough to make even the most mild-mannered of person consider uttering something stronger than 'blimey'.

With a growl, he crushed the note, the paper crumpling like dry leaves beneath a boot heal. That Lister had orchestrated this chaos as a mere diversion—a prelude to what he planned at the wedding—sent waves of frustration pulsing through Peter. Yet, amidst the tumult of emotions, a steely resolve took root.

'Damn it,' Peter muttered. 'He won't win this game.'

The lines around his eyes hardened, his usual affable demeanour momentarily eclipsed. Lyn owned a steeliness that he admired; she wouldn't bend to fear, and neither would he. It wasn't about their safety anymore. They wanted to protect the peacefulness of their village from Lister's harmful actions.

'Lister's going to pay for this,' Peter declared, more to himself than to Jemma.

With the remnants of the mocking note still clutched in his fist, Peter's mind whirred into action. There was no time for self-pity; he had a wedding to protect, and a cunning adversary to outfox.

His gaze snapped from the crumpled paper to Jemma, who was still blinking away the cobwebs of unconsciousness. 'Jemma,' he said, his voice uncharacteristically sharp. 'What do you know about Lister's plans?'

'Plans?' Jemma echoed; her voice groggy. She looked like a startled barn owl caught in the headlights of a fast approaching car. 'I—I just delivered messages, that's all. Fetch this, carry that. I never knew...' Her words trailed off into uncertainty.

'Think, Jemma,' Peter urged with impatience. 'Anything he said. Places he mentioned? People he met?'

Jemma shook her head, her confusion as genuine as the wrinkles on Phyllis' stockings. 'He's always been secretive. Just told me what to do, never why. I thought it was all... a game.'

'Right, a deadly game of hide and seek,' Peter muttered

to himself. He felt frustration bubbling inside him like a kettle ready to whistle. Jemma was a dead end—a fact as clear as the Norfolk sky on a frost-laden night.

Peter paced back and forth, the debris crunching underfoot. His thoughts flitted from one possibility to the next like a swallow darting through the air. Who else could provide a clue to Lister's whereabouts? The village was small; secrets were usually as well-kept as a hedgehog in a library. Yet, Lister had slipped through their fingers like an eel in the Bure River.

'Think, Peter, think!' he chided himself. He needed a lead, something solid to go on. His gaze wandered to the tranquil countryside, unaware of the sinister plot unfolding beneath its surface.

'Could Phyllis know something?' he wondered aloud. The woman had ears that could detect a whisper in a hurricane. Yet her information was often as reliable as a chocolate teapot. He quickly dismissed the idea; time was too precious to chase Phyllis's wild goose stories.

A plan formed in Peter's mind, as delicate and intricate as lacework. He needed to tap into the village grapevine, discreetly. There had to be someone out there with a snippet of overheard conversation, a sighting that didn't fit, anything that could point them towards Lister.

'Jemma,' he said, more gently now, 'you're caught up in something much bigger than errands. Stay here, the officers will look after you.' He offered her a reassuring pat on the shoulder before turning to leave.

'There's... something else.'

Peter frowned when he caught her worried look. 'Something else? What do you mean? Is there something you're not telling me?'

'He has a gun,' Jemma blurted, her eyes cast downwards, unable to meet her visitor's gaze.

'But how? Did you get the weapon for him, Jemma?' Peter's demeanour hardened at news of a dangerous adversary carrying a deadly weapon.

'No,' Jemma shouted, her eyes fixed on Peter's. 'I... I couldn't help myself. When he was out one day, I rummaged through the drawers in his bedroom, and there it was. I took a picture on my mobile and looked it up online. It's a Beretta pistol. Does that mean anything to you?'

'All two well, I'm afraid. I'll bet my cap on it being the Link Series 4.'

'Is that bad?'

'About as bad as it can get for a sidearm.'

Peter raised his look to the ceiling, closed his eyes, and sighed. On top of everything else, he now had an armed assailant on the run with a state-of-the-art weapon.

Forcing himself back to reality, he made for the stairs, then crossed the tiny vestibule before opening the front door.

'Be careful, Peter,' Jemma called after him, her voice laced with concern.

Without looking back, Peter stepped out into the sunshine and headed for his car. As the early afternoon wore on, so did the urgency to unravel Lister's nefarious scheme before it reached its crescendo at Ant and Lyn's wedding.

'Lister,' Peter mused with a grim smile, 'it's time to bring this to an end.'

The quaint English countryside, usually a postcard of serenity, now played host to the chaotic aftermath of Lister's latest gambit. As he drove away from the chocolate-box cottage, the bright sunlight bathed the hedgerows in a warm glow, an ironic contrast to the cold fury simmering within him. He had to protect Ant and Lyn, come hell or high water.

'Right,' Peter muttered to himself, 'Time to think again.'

The engine hummed to life, and he drove back to the station, leaves dancing in the wake of his departure.

Upon arriving at the police station, Peter found it buzzing like a hive after a bear's unwelcome visit. His team huddled around desks littered with maps and take-away coffee cups, a signal of long hours spent on the case. With a brisk nod, he summoned them into the briefing room.

'Listen up,' Peter began, urgency creeping into his voice as he scanned their attentive faces. 'No time for an inquest now how Lister escaped. I will say one thing, though. There are actors in and around the village that decided our prisoner had to be sprung from his cell. None of you are to blame for what happened. Do you understand?'

Confused glances swept the room at the ragged sight their superior presented. No one had the courage to ask what had happened. For now, it was enough to ensure their superior's words sank in.

'Any luck with that other prisoner?' Peter asked, keen to change the subject.

After a brief pause, an officer spoke up. 'Good as gold, Guv,' Sergeant Harris said, a pencil tucked behind his ear. 'Though he fancies himself the next celebrity criminal, keeps going on about how famous he's going to be.'

'Is that right?' Peter mused aloud, eyes narrowing. 'Let me have a quick word with our star-in-waiting.' Peter turned to the desk sergeant and handed him the slip of paper Siegfried had furnished him with. 'arrange for a forensic team to get there and two constables to establish a sterile zone around the building.'

The sergeant looked at the paper slip, then back at his superior. 'Should I call the mortuary, too?'

'No, although they will find a dazed young lady present. You'll need to bring her in for questioning, but tell them to be gentle with her. She's just been blown up.'

'Blown... '

'No time to explain now. I'll sort it out later.'

Peter left a dazed-looking sergeant as he approached the cells where the self-proclaimed mastermind awaited. The man sat on a stone shelf covered with a thin mattress, legs bouncing with nervous energy.

'Morning—or is it afternoon?' Peter said in greeting, his tone casual. 'Tell me all about your big plans. Must be quite the scheme if you're this chuffed about it.'

'Ah, you know, it's all about timing and... uh... execution.' The man's voice trailed off, his bravado deflating like a pricked balloon.

'Go on then,' Peter coaxed, leaning against the heavy cell door with feigned interest. 'Impress me.'

The man continued talking about grandeur and fame. However, it became obvious he knew little about Lister's plans. A fantasist through and through.

'Right, that's enough for one day,' Peter said, cutting the man off mid-sentence. He slammed the cell door behind him and beckoned to the desk sergeant. 'Cut him loose, but make sure someone drives him to North Walsham. Don't need him clouding the waters here.'

'Will do, Guv,' the sergeant replied.

'Make sure he gets the message: no more crying wolf, or he'll be breaking stones at His Majesty's glee,' Peter added, his tone leaving no room for argument.

With their would-be celebrity dispatched, Peter returned to his team. There they sat, ready to piece together the fractured puzzle of Lister's whereabouts, before the clock ticked any closer to Ant and Lyn's nuptials.

The conference room at the station was a buzz of tension. Maps of Norfolk splayed across the table like a gambler's last hand. Peter stood at the head, tapping a pen against his notepad as he eyed his officers.

'Lister's no fool; he'll avoid the obvious places,' he began, voice low but carrying. 'But he'll still be local, that's for sure.'

The jovial banter, which usually accompanied their strategy sessions, had evaporated. Now grim determination filled the room.

'Keep your eyes peeled- and be discreet,' Peter instructed as he scanned the faces before him. 'Last thing we need is panic spreading around the village.'

A murmur rippled through the team. They knew the stakes—protecting the village's heart and soul wasn't just duty; it was personal.

'Right, let's move. Double up patrols and keep your radios close,' Peter concluded, the urgency clear in his tone.

With nods of assent, the officers dispersed, each carrying a slice of the burden. Peter lingered, collecting his thoughts before heading to the church to oversee the final security sweep.

The quaint stone building, usually a picture of peace, now loomed like a question mark against the Norfolk skyline. The vicar greeted him with a nervous smile, wringing his hands as if trying to squeeze out the last drops of calm.

'Everything's set for the wedding, Peter,' he said, his voice laced with forced cheer.

'Good, good,' Peter replied, his gaze drifting to the back of the church. He caught sight of a police dog handler was making the rounds with his charge, a keen-eyed labrador named Jasper.

'Find anything interesting, boy?' Peter called out lightly, hoping to lift the strained atmosphere.

Jasper wagged his tail but remained resolutely seated in front of the ancient font. The handler knelt, examining what Jasper had taken an interest in.

'Sir, he's indicating...' the handler began, his voice trailing off.

Peter's heart skipped a beat. 'Oh no, not now, Jasper,' he muttered.

He joined the handler, peering at the carved stone font. People were trickling in, their cheerful chatter an uneasy contrast to his sudden spike of adrenaline.

'Anything?' Peter asked.

The sound of guests drowned the handler's reply, their laughter echoing off the stone walls. The vicar, unaware of the unfolding drama, welcomed them with open arms.

'Sir...' the handler started again, his voice tense.

'Out with it, man,' Peter urged, his face draining of colour as he imagined the unthinkable.

'Jasper's never wrong about these things,' the handler said, his face solemn.

As the sun traced past high noon, a narrow shaft of light pierced the open church door, its journey cut short by the ancient font. Peter could only hope they weren't too late.

Peter leaned in, the dampness of the stone seeping through his fingers as he brushed them over Jasper's find. His breath hitched in his throat as he discovered a carefully concealed seam on the font's edge. There it was: an intricately designed hatch, cleverly hidden within the ancient carvings.

With the church continuing to fill with guests, their

Sunday best brushing against the pews, Peter's heart thudded with a new rhythm—dread. He had a decision to make. Did he evacuate the church and cause chaos, or say nothing, leaving each guest that passed the font to give him a curious look, but nothing more? 'Thirty-seconds, that's all I need,' Peter whispered.

'Okay,' he said, trying to sound cheerful, 'let's take a quick look before the bride comes, alright?'

He wiggled the hatch open. A stream of Anglo-Saxon curses ran through his mind, each more colourful than the last. Inside lay an object wrapped in Prestine red velvet. The church bells rang in the background. The dissonance between their happy chorus and Peter's predicament could not have been greater.

As Peter reached for the velvet-wrapped mystery, Jasper let out a low growl, his ears flat against his head. The air seemed to still as, with one swift movement, Peter unveiled their find.

Jasper's warning growls and the joyous hubbub of the wedding guests drowned Peter's own heavy breathing out. The object revealed wasn't just another clue—it was something far more dire. Just as his fingers grazed it, a single, low note from the church organ relaced the previous joyous chorus as it reverberated through the church. Every surface seemed to shudder.

The hook of Lister's theme tune hummed ominously in the air.

Chapter Thirteen

FRIENDSHIPS IN PERIL

Saturday, 6th September 2.00 pm

PETER'S HANDS shook as he carefully uncovered the hidden item from the old font. The memory card dropped on the stone floor in the silent church with a click. He crouched to retrieve it, noting how Jasper, the police dog, seemed to grow more eager with every step nearer to the deceptive fabric.

'Steady on, Jasper,' cautioned the dog's handler, alarm in his voice. 'There's a faint smell here... Smells like plastic explosives.'

'Fiendish, isn't he?' Peter mumbled, his jaw tightening at the thought of Lister's cunning. It was a narrow escape, too close. They could have been moments away from an evacuation—or worse.

With the memory card now secure between his fingers, Peter dashed over to one of the church's side benches and pulled out his Samsung mobile. His thumb pressed hard against the tiny piece of technology as he slotted it into the phone's port. His heart pounded with impatience while the data loaded, each second stretching out like an eternity.

The file opened, and Peter scanned the series of photographs. Each one was a close-up—a segment of a larger, hidden reality. He knew this was Lister at his most cryptic; there had to be a connection, a thread weaving through the chaos. And then, amid the disjointed images, something caught his eye.

The detective zoomed in on a photo displaying an elegant table setting, and there, etched onto a silver fork handle, was a crest. The lines and curves of the emblem leaped out at him as he enlarged the image. A lightning bolt of realisation struck. The Stanton family crest. It was undeniable.

'Of course,' he whispered to himself, his mind racing as he flicked back through the other photos. Each random shot took on a new significance. The wedding reception at Stanton Hall—it linked them all together.

'Lister, you've set the stage, but I intend to close the curtain,' Peter declared, a smile momentarily breaking through his frustration. With newfound resolve, he pocketed his phone, ready to piece together the fragments of Lister's twisted plan.

Peter's hands trembled as he turned to the police dog handler, a wiry man, his face etched with concern. 'Keep Jasper on a tight leash outside,' he instructed crisply. 'We can't risk transmitting anything on the radios—Lister might be listening in.'

The handler nodded, understanding flashing in his eyes. He gripped Jasper's lead more firmly, the Labrador's ears twitching with alertness.

'Go around and inform the others—face to face, mind you—keep it quiet. Maintain a radio silence until I give the word, or unless you spot that slippery eel Lister first,' Peter continued, his voice low but intense.

'Got it, boss,' the handler replied, patting Jasper's head before moving off with purposeful strides, the dog eagerly pulling ahead.

Peter dashed out of the church and into his unmarked police car, his mind whirring with scenarios and strategies. Ignoring the siren and lights, which would serve only to announce his approach to a man as cunning as Lister, he drove through the narrow country lanes. His driving was erratic, a mirror to his thoughts, as he weaved between hedgerows and fences that bordered the winding roads of rural Norfolk.

Approaching Stanton Hall, Peter's foot pressed hard on the brakes, the tyres screeching in protest as he stopped just shy of the open entrance gates. He stepped out, taking a moment to survey the grandeur of the estate, its facade both imposing and serene amidst the pastoral landscape.

Just as Peter was about to slip through a discreet trail, a field officer appeared and disrupted his plan.

'Stand down,' the officer barked, his hand raised in a halting gesture. 'You've orders to leave Lister alone.'

Peter locked eyes, jaw clenching in frustration. His opponent's stance remained unwavering; a sign he was not to be trifled with. Peter considered his next move. He couldn't risk compromising their operation. Then again, he didn't have time to waste.

'Look, I understand orders. Hey, let's start again. You know who I am. What do I call you?'

The man gave Riley a quizzical look before he let his guard down a notch. 'It's Mike, but it doesn't change things.'

'Thanks, Mike. I get that, but Lister poses a significant

threat. 'The wedding must take place unhindered by a crazy loner. Wait too long and who knows what he'll get up to?'

'Orders are orders,' Mike said in a flat tone.

'I appreciate your situation, but look at things from my point of view. I have to get to Lister before he steps foot in Stanton Hall,' he insisted, thrusting his smartphone screen towards the officer. The images flickered under the dappled shade of the trees.

Mike didn't look. 'You aren't going anywhere near Lister.'

Peter's frustration simmered. He recognised the need to be cautious. The detective took breathed deeply to steady his nerves; he attempted a different approach.

'Listen, we can't afford to underestimate Lister's capabilities. Lives are at stake,' Peter implored.

The officer remained stoic, unmoved by Peter's plea. However, a flicker of interest crossed his features as he glanced at the screen image.

Peter seized this momentary crack in the officer's amour. 'If we wait too long, it might be too late,' he emphasised.

After a pregnant pause, Mike relented.

'Look,' Peter said, pointing at the Stanton family crest etched onto the silverware in the picture. 'This isn't just a wild goose chase Lister has set; it's a meticulously planned trap.'

'We have eyes on Lister, Peter. He's still prancing around the grounds like he owns the place, but he hasn't made a move towards the Hall.'

'Prancing?' Peter echoed, the word leaving a sour taste in his mouth. 'He's a predator, not an eager deer.'

'That may be,' Mike continued, 'we're keeping him under surveillance. No one is in danger. We have the situation under complete control.'

'Complete control?' Peter scoffed, folding his arms. 'The last time we thought we had him in check, I almost evacuated the church.'

'I note your concern, Detective,' replied the officer, remaining as motionless as a statue. 'But you will stand down. Those are the orders.'

Peter's mind raced. He couldn't defy direct orders, but the thought of Lister slipping through their fingers filled him with dread. The wedding hung in the balance, and Peter couldn't shake the urgency gnawing at him.

A plan formed in Peter's mind. He needed to outmanoeuvre Lister without openly disobeying his orders. He straightened his posture and locked eyes with Mike.

'Orders,' he muttered. His gaze drifting past the officer to where the grandeur of Stanton Hall rested, its windows reflecting the waning light like eyes full of secrets.

'Fine,' he said, the word clipped and final. As he turned, a spark of rebellion flared within him, as unpredictable and fierce as one of Lyn Blackthorn's resolute decisions. Protocol might momentarily cage him. However, Peter had his escape plan.

'Surveillance,' he muttered, his lips curling around the word with disdain. It was as if they were observing a rare bird prancing in the underbrush, not a man like Lister—a sly fox that could dart away at the slightest rustle.

The hush of Norfolk's countryside mocked him. The wisps of clouds above drifted lazily, indifferent to the urgency pulsating in Peter's veins. He could hear Phyllis, the town gossip, scolding him for being impatient, her words as suffocating as Betty's strong lavender perfume.

He couldn't just stand by. 'Think, think,' he coached himself, his mind a whirlpool of conflicting currents. On one hand, Lister was a serpent in the grass, his fangs poised to strike. To ignore that threat would be folly. But orders were orders, even when they stank worse than a forgotten kipper beneath a choir pew.

A blackbird took flight from a nearby hedge, its wings slicing through the tension like a well-aimed dart. In its ascent, Peter found a flicker of clarity. The countess, with her keen eyes that missed nothing, would understand the necessity of strategy over brute force. He had to be cunning, a shadow moving unseen, rather than the blunt instrument he so longed to employ.

'Patience,' he whispered, the words a balm to his churning thoughts. It was a game of wits now, a battle of stealth against the ticking clock of Lister's machinations. Despite every fibre rebelling against the order to stand down, he knew that sometimes silence allowed for the boldest moves.

As he strode away, his steps measured but purposeful, he cast one last glance over his shoulder. Mike remained steadfast, a sentinel guarding a truth only Peter felt brewing. With a shake of his head, the detective conceded this round to the chain of command—but the match wasn't over.

Peter's steps offered a steady drumbeat as he retreated to his car. He knew that just as anticipation hummed in the air like bees around a bloom. The church would soon be full to the brim with villagers. All waiting to greet the bride and groom for their grand affair.

'Not beaten yet,' he mumbled, adjusting the rear-view mirror as if to affirm the decision for his own reflection. 'Keep your friends close, and your suspects closer.'

His police car navigated the winding lanes with an intimacy born of years patrolling his beat. The hedgerows flashed by; a blur of green speckled with the white blossoms of wildflowers. To any onlooker, it was just another day in

Norfolk. But beneath the idyllic surface, a game of cat and mouse played out, its stakes life and death.

Rounding a bend, the Hall rose in all its magnificence, its walls a fortress in the landscape. Peter's eyes caught on a feature he'd been looking out for—a gate partially concealed by an overgrowth of ivy and briars. It whispered opportunity to his seasoned instincts.

In one swift motion, he steered the car onto the grass verge, parking it behind a stand of trees where it would go unseen. Peter eyed the gate. He was a man unaccustomed to taking orders when his gut screamed otherwise.

'Sorry, fella,' he said, addressing the absent field officer as he exited the vehicle. 'But I've got to do it.'

The gate protested with a metallic groan as his hands forced it open, the rusted hinges betraying years of neglect. He looked back at the lane to make sure he was alone. Then, he slipped through the gap and closed the gate behind him, fully committed to this unconventional path.

'Steady now,' he coached himself, the verdant wall of the estate standing at attention to his solitary infiltration. 'In for a penny, in for a pound.'

He adjusted his tie, a touch of sartorial armour, and set off with the stealth of a fox. A dash of humour warming his thoughts despite the gravity of the mission. For in the dance of danger and wit, he knew there was no partner more reliable than a dose of village cunning.

Peter's shoes sank into the soft loam of the woodland floor, his progress a careful ballet between shadow and silence. To his left, barely visible through the tangle of bracken, the glint of a field officer's binoculars betrayed their vigilance. He crouched behind a gnarled oak, heart pounding in time with the jays that scolded overhead, their raucous cries a diversion he silently thanked.

'Right,' he whispered to himself, 'if Lister can slip through their fingers, so can I.'

Peter's form seamlessly blended with the dappling sunlight, casting a mosaic of light and shadow. He attuned his senses to every rustle, every bird call, every fleeting movement in the underbrush.

As he navigated the wooded expanse, Peter couldn't help but marvel at the symphony of nature around him.

Moving cautiously, his determination became a powerful force that pushed him forward. The stakes were high, but Peter thrived in the adrenaline-charged atmosphere of uncertainty.

The trees thinned, and Peter found himself at the forest's edge. The rear of Stanton Hall loomed across the pristine lawn, its windows like eyes that watched for intruders. One hundred yards of open ground lay between him and the grand building—a no-man's-land that could make or break his covert assault.

'Dash it all,' he muttered, eyeing the distance. A hare shot across the lawn, swift and unnoticed. 'If he can do it, so can I.'

Peter hunched low, his form a mere shadow against the lush backdrop of manicured lawns and imposing brick façade. The Hall stood as a silent sentinel to his daring intrusion, its stones seeming to warn of the danger that lurked within. But a determination that burned bright, undeterred by the barriers that stood in his path.

With a last glance over his shoulder, he steeled himself for the sprint across the open expanse. The sun, high in the sky, cast momentary shadows that danced across the grass like fleeting spectres. Peter took a deep breath, the air cool, and crisp against his skin, before launching into a sprint that carried him towards the Hall like a bullet from a gun.

His heart thundered; each beat a drumroll of anticipation as he closed the distance with rapid strides. The world around him seemed to blur, colours melding into a whirl of green and brown as he focused solely on the building at his front.

His feet pounded the turf, the hall growing ever closer with each stride. He felt a surge of triumph—until a root, camouflaged by the neatly trimmed grass, caught his ankle. Peter tumbled forward, the world turning over as he rolled to a stop just shy of the hall's majestic steps.

'Blimey,' he gasped, winded but acutely aware of the rustle of pursuit.

Before he could gather his wits, a firm hand clamped down on Peter's shoulder, hauling him up with surprising strength. Peter blinked, clearing his vision, and shocked to stare at the last person he thought he would see on this secret mission.

'Anthony?' he spluttered, disbelief colouring his tone as he took in the sight of his friend dressed in an immaculate morning suit, with a button-hole red rose. A combination of concern and confusion replaced his usual composed demeanour.

'What on earth are you doing here, Peter?' Ant asked in a hushed tone. If it's about Lister, I thought you said he's safely locked up at the police station?'

Peter shook his head, attempting to regain his composure as he scrambled to his feet, brushing off stray blades of grass from his rumpled clothes. 'It's complicated,' Peter said, still catching his breath from his tumble.

Peter tried to gather his thoughts, the encounter with Ant catching him off guard in more ways than one. His mind raced to find a plausible explanation that wouldn't compromise the delicate balance of trust he had built with Ant over the years.

'Anthony, I can't divulge all the details just yet,' Peter began cautiously, choosing his words with care. 'Let's just say that there have been some recent developments that require me to be here, off the record.'

Ant frowned, his gaze searching Peter's face for answers. 'Off the record? Peter, you know I trust you implicitly, but secrets have a way of unravelling at the most inopportune moments.'

Peter nodded, acknowledging Ant's point. 'I understand your apprehension, Anthony. But believe me when I say that what I'm doing is necessary.'

'You didn't answer me when I asked if Lister was in your jail, Peter. Is he?'

'I can't lie to you. No. He isn't. In fact, he's somewhere on your grounds.'

Ant's face contorted with confusion. 'You mean you don't know where he is? And how does that leave the wedding? I leave for the church in ten minutes. Trust is one thing, Peter, but when it comes to Lyn's safety, I need more than that.'

Peter watched Ant's face contort from confusion to grim determination.

'Anthony, I can only offer you trust now. This, along with the promise that undercover agents are in place throughout the Hall and grounds to ensure everyone's safety.'

'Agents? That's an odd way of putting things. What is it you are not telling me? Lyn and I deserve more than verbal gymnastics, don't you think?'

A voice shouting after Ant broke the moment. In seconds, the earl appeared at the door from where Ant stood. 'The Rolls is waiting for you at the main entrance. You must leave for the church-now!'

Peter and Ant exchanged stern looks.

'This isn't over, Peter,' Ant remarked with a coldness to his voice.

Peter didn't reply. Instead, he felt a hard-earned friend-ship careering into oblivion.

Chapter Fourteen

READY OR NOT

Saturday, 6th September 2.45 pm

ANT STOOD SILENTLY in the quiet of St. Peter's churchyard, his fingers tracing the cold marble of the headstone that bore his brother's name. The cloudless skies above were at odds with the sombreness of the moment.

'Greg,' he murmured, voice barely rising above the rustling leaves. 'I'm getting married today, big brother. You should be here, fumbling with the rings; teasing me about tripping over Lyn's train.' Ant paused, the importance of the day urging him on. 'I miss you, mate. There's so much I want to tell you. So much you would have loved about today. I wish you were walking beside me, ready to crack one of your daft jokes.'

With a last pat on the cold stone, Ant rose, straightened his tie and morning suit with a nervous chuckle. 'Well, can't keep the lady waiting, can I? She's got enough to worry about without me turning up late. Keep an eye out for us, yeah?'

Shaking off the melancholy, Ant strode towards the church, the ancient oak door wide open to reveal a sight that stopped him in his tracks. The small village church, usually half-empty for Sunday service, struggled to seat everybody. Every pew filled with expectant faces, a sea of smiles and new clothes bought especially for the day. More than that, an air of barely contained excitement that hummed like bees in a hive.

'Blimey,' Ant whispered, a broad grin spreading across his face as he stepped into the warm embrace of the congregation.

'Anthony!' Phyllis, the village gossip, waved a gloved hand from her perch. He smiled inwardly at her trademark dark attire and her hat adorned with a stuffed bird that looked as if it were falling off its perch. 'You look dapper! And on time too - an omen, I'd wager!'

'Thank you, Phyllis,' Ant replied, his laughter bubbling up. 'I'll take any omens you've got tucked away in that hat of yours.'

As he made his way down the aisle, shaking hands and sharing hugs, Ant couldn't help but marvel at the kaleido-scope of humanity gathered in one place. The Squire's wife, Mrs. Havering, fluttered her fan dramatically, while the local baker promised a wedding cake that would be the talk of Norfolk for years to come.

'Ant, dear boy!' called out Mrs. Havering, her voice carrying over the hubbub. 'Don't you go keeping that lovely girl waiting now!'

'Wouldn't dream of it, Mrs. Havering,' Ant replied. He thought of Lyn, the woman who stole his heart, with their shared love for the quirks of Stanton Parva and the growing mysteries in their corner of England.

'Today's going to be perfect,' he whispered to himself,

with a confidence that felt more certain with every step he took towards the front of the church. In the warmth of the gathered crowd and the soft glow of the stained glass, Ant knew Greg couldn't be there. The love and laughter of the day would honour his memory in the most beautiful way possible.

Settling into the front pew, Ant caught Fitch's eye and leaned in for a conspiratorial whisper. 'Can you believe it? The day is finally here.'

'Believe it?' Fitch grinned, adjusting his cufflinks with a flourish. 'I've heard nothing else about today for months!'

'Ah, but you love being part of all the drama,' Ant teased, nudging his friend's shoulder. 'Admit it, you're as much a sucker for this stuff as I am.'

'Guilty as charged,' Fitch confessed with a chuckle. 'But today, it's all about you and Lyn. Ready to make it official?'

'More than ready,' Ant replied, his gaze drifting over the assembly of friends, family, and familiar faces that made up the gathering. Each one was like a thread in the tapestry of their lives, woven together in shared history and affection.

The first notes of the wedding march resonated through the church, commanding the attention of every soul present. The congregation rose in unison, an undulating sea of pastel hats and polished shoes, turning towards the back of the church expectantly.

There, beneath the archway of blooming lilies and ivy, stood Lyn, a vision in white. Her gown cascaded down in layers of delicate lace and silk, hugging her slender frame before flaring into a graceful train. Her blond hair swept up elegantly, a few tendrils escaping to frame her radiant face. It was the sort of dress that whispered rather than shouted its splendour, much like the woman who wore it.

Ant felt something catch in his throat, a mixture of awe

and elation, as he watched Lyn begin her procession down the aisle, her arm looped through her father's. The proud, tender smile he wore, guiding his beloved daughter with a gentle steadiness towards her new life softened his nervous bearing.

As Lyn drew closer, Ant's heart thrummed, a rhythmic echo to the organ's melody. Now he could see the sparkle in her eyes, the same unwavering spirit that had charmed him from their very first encounter as children. She was the puzzle piece that fitted seamlessly into his life, the answer to riddles he hadn't known he'd been asking.

The light from the stained-glass windows made Lyn look beautiful, and it created pretty shadows on the flower petals strewn in her way. Ant thought fleetingly of the wild-flowers they both loved. How they bloomed unexpectedly, bringing beauty to even the most hidden corners of Norfolk. Lyn was his wildflower, resilient and bright against any backdrop.

'Stunning,' Fitch murmured, voicing the sentiment clear on every face in the church.

'Wow,' Ant gasped, his gaze fixed on Lyn as if she were the only person in the room. As she neared, his anticipation swelled, a joyous crescendo that filled the solemn space.

Their connection was palpable, a silent promise of adventure and mystery that lay ahead, wrapped in the comforting embrace of the village. This was their moment, a new chapter written with love and the occasional dash of intrigue.

As Reverend Morton cleared his throat, a hush fell over the congregation. Ant stood at the altar, his hands trembling, not from nerves but from sheer emotion at what was about to be shared. He turned toward Lyn, whose smile was as reassuring as it was radiant. The ancient church, with its stone walls and timbered roof, seemed to lean in, intent on witnessing the vows of this beloved couple.

'Anthony, James, Alfred Stanton,' the Reverend began, the formality of his tone belying the mischief in his eye, 'do you take Lynette, Jane Blackthorn to be your lawfully wedded wife, to have and to hold, from this day forward, for better, for worse, for richer, for poorer, in sickness and in health, until death do you part?'

Ant's voice was firm, carrying through the church like a beacon. 'I do,' he declared, looking into Lyn's eyes, which sparkled with unshed tears and laughter. 'And I vow to cherish every mystery and joy we encounter together.'

Lyn's lips quirked into a playful grin, knowing full well the adventures that awaited them. 'And I,' she said, her voice strong, 'take you, Anthony, James, Alfred Stanton, to be my husband. To laugh with you in triumph, to console you when our clues lead us astray, and to stand by you as we unravel life's meandering roads.'

The exchange of rings followed, each band glinting like a promise under the soft light filtering through the stained glass. They turned to face their friends and family, their union sealed with a kiss. As they did so, the church erupted in applause, a cascade of cheer that echoed off the walls and out into the lush surroundings of Norfolk.

Saturday, 6th September 2.45 pm

PETER, still reeling from Ant's accusation of failed trust, entered the grandeur of Stanton Hall. He hurried along a wide corridor, the afternoon sun casting long shadows into the voluminous space. The Great Hall revealed itself just ahead, its enormous floor space busy with final preparations for the upcoming reception.

Staff bustled with efficiency. Florists arranging centre-pieces with delicate care; caterers wheeling in trolleys laden with culinary delights, and the housekeeping team adding final touches to the decor. The air resonated with a symphony of clinking glasses; silverware being polished. In charge of all stood and the instructions of David, the butler, orchestrating the scene.

Peter surveyed the hall, noting the strategic placement of exits and the flow of service paths. His mind, ever attuned to potential danger. He catalogued each detail, storing the information for a situation he hoped would never arise. Yet, amid his vigilance, he couldn't help but let a small smile play upon his lips; the spirit of celebration was infectious, and even he, with all his caution, felt the pull of joy that today represented.

His gaze lingered on the soaring ceilings where banners and ribbons fluttered gently in the breeze from the open windows. They danced merrily, as if in tune with the larks that called to each other in the waning afternoon. In this moment, the hall was not just a setting for revelry, but a testament to village life. A place where stories unfolded, and history honoured.

As Peter's footsteps echoed on the marble floor, he allowed himself a brief respite. Today was a day of union, of love triumphing, and of mysteries put aside for the cele-bration of two souls entwined.

The cutlery rested with military precision on the tables, a parade of silver glinting under the warm glow of the chandeliers. The chatter of the staff was a hushed hum as they scurried about, adding last-minute touches to the Great

Hall. Peter paced the perimeter, his eyes sharp and search-ing. A detective at heart amid domesticity on a grand scale.

'David,' he called out softly to the butler, who appeared as if conjured from the very air—dignified, discreet, and impossibly efficient. 'A moment, if you please.'

'Of course, Detective Inspector,' David replied, moving with the grace of a swan navigating the village pond. His expression was an unreadable mask of professionalism. The sort that had seen more secrets than the local vicar's confessional.

'Have there been any... unusual visitors today? Someone not on the guest list or staff rota?' Peter asked, keeping his voice low enough to blend with the rustling of the floral arrangements.

David's eyes betrayed nothing as he shook his head, his posture as straight as the steeple at St. Peter's church where vows were being exchanged. 'I can assure you, sir, Stanton Hall has welcomed only those with invitations penned by the lovely couple themselves. As for the staff, no one has entered without my seeing and recognising them.'

'Keep a weather eye open, will you?' Peter urged, his tone light but the look in his eyes serious. 'You know of whom I speak when I say he has a habit of turning up like a bad penny. Unwanted and decidedly dangerous.'

'Indeed, sir.' David's lips twitched imperceptibly, as if the idea of Lister gatecrashing the event was as likely as the King popping by for tea unannounced. 'We shall remain vigilant.'

'Appreciate it,' Peter said with a nod, stepping back to allow the butler to continue with his duties. He trusted the butler, of course; the man could spot a speck of dust on a chandelier from forty paces. But Lister's arrogance was the stuff of legend, akin to the tales of old that filled Norfolk's pubs—larger-than-life and twice as cunning.

As he stood fixed to the spot. He imagined the scene when Ant and Lyn arrived, followed by the principal guests within the hour. A room full of joy, yet with danger just a heartbeat away.

Peter, brought back to reality by a member of staff dropping a tray of glasses, cast another critical eye over the grandeur of the Great Hall. The room continued to hum with activity. Candles flickered on silver candelabras, casting a warm glow on oak-panelled walls. Outside, the afternoon sun draped the rolling Norfolk landscape in a golden shroud.

'Only Lister would dare spoil such a splendid affair,' Peter muttered. His mind raced, like a chess player planning several moves ahead. He imagined the fallen commander moving stealthily among the people, seeking the sick pleasure of spreading chaos in a joyful setting.

'Every rose has its thorn, eh?' Peter thought. He pictured Lyn's serene smile, how she'd turned the village school around with her unwavering resolve and now stood at the precipice of wedded bliss. 'And every wedding has a Lister, of sorts.'

He paced along the edges of the room, nodding at the occasional well-wisher who mistook his vigilance for prenuptial nerves. Peter passed by a table weighed down with gifts wrapped in glossy paper and ribbon, a testament to the community's affection for the couple. His attention pivoted momentarily to two elderly staff debating the merits of fruitcake versus sponge for matrimonial confectionery. This was a debate, he noted, of equal importance to the whereabouts of international criminals as far as they were concerned.

'Focus, Peter,' he chided himself, redirecting his focus to the task at hand. He visualised the event's timeline. Drinks on arrival, the meal, speeches, first dance. He tried to pinpoint areas of vulnerability. It was an impossible task to check every nook, every shadowed corner that offered concealment. Yet, it was not the physical spaces that concerned him most. It was the theatricality of the disruption that would appeal to a man like Lister.

'Wanting to witness the fruits of your villainy first hand?' Peter pondered. He almost admired the audacity it would take to stand amidst the victims undetected. It was a dangerous game of hide and seek. Peter felt a shiver of anticipation snake up his spine despite himself. He knew Lister would breach any security. 'But why sneak yourself into a room you plan to destroy? Surely, you'd put your own life in danger. And I know you are no hero,' Peter mused.

The thought left Peter with the notion that two scenarios were at play. Either Lister had already planted the seeds of destruction in the room, or he timed his attack on when Ant and Lyn arrived or left the reception.

Peter made a muted promise, balancing the danger with the celebratory mood. It was a balancing act only a man with his set of skills could manage. And with the stage set for celebration, Peter knew the next act would be one of cunning and resolve.

Inching closer to an elaborate ice sculpture—a swan poised mid-preen—Peter's finger traced the cool surface. He contemplated his next move. He couldn't shake the feeling that Lister was near, watching him fumble in this game of cat-and-mouse.

'Need eyes everywhere,' he concluded, his thoughts rapidly coalescing into action. It was time to call in reinforcements, despite the personal cost it might incur. Being reprimanded or stood down by his superiors was a trivial price to pay if it meant safeguarding the newlyweds and their guests.

'Time to stir things up.' He knew he had to find one of the suited gentleman's spies who was currently observing Lister on the grounds for their own agenda. He allowed his mind to race. What if they wanted Lister to try something? Wouldn't that put him in deeper debt to them if they got him away—to blackmail him into doing even more nefarious work for them?

'Stop it,' Peter chided himself, recognising how ridiculous he was being... or was he? He couldn't get the idea out of his head. Ant had told him one or two things over the years about intelligence agencies. He'd said that if a mission were important enough, the officers would receive orders to do whatever was necessary to accomplish their mission. The suited gentleman that Peter met at the old forge hadn't said what Lister's mission was before he went rogue to harm Ant and Lyn. What if that mission fell into the definition of, 'do what you have to do?'

Still, Peter had no choice. He had to contact them to stop whatever it was Lister had planned.

Either way, the die was cast. As the rural landscape embraced Stanton Hall in its timeless grip, Peter played his last card. To set the trap, he had to get at least one intelligence officer to help him. Peter refused to contemplate the awful alternative ending to the day's events.

Chapter Fifteen

SMOKE WITHOUT MIRRORS

Saturday, 6th September 3.20 pm

PETER CREPT THROUGH THE UNDERGROWTH, leaves rustling softly beneath his cautious steps. The grandeur of Norfolk's landscape, lost on him now, as he pursued a far more pressing matter than admiring the wildlife. He looked around the wooded area near Stanton Hall, searching for any signs of a hidden intelligence officer.

'Mustn't startle Lister,' Peter muttered to himself, aware that if the villain caught wind of his presence, it could spell disaster for Ant and Lyn. He paused, holding his breath, trying to pick out any human disturbance from the symphony of nature.

Abruptly, a hand landed on Peter's shoulder like the weighty judgement of a disapproving aunt. His heart leapt into his throat. With adrenaline coursing through his veins, he wondered if Lister had somehow circled back without him noticing.

He whirled around to face the intruder, ready to

confront or flee. Instead of the menacing figure of Lister, Peter's glance settled on an intelligence officer. The stern yet familiar features of Siegfried, the same intelligence officer who had spoken to him earlier.

'Remember me? I told you to stand down,' the officer whispered, his eyes scanning the area just as intently as Peter had been moments before.

'Blimey, give a fellow a warning!' Peter exclaimed, attempting to regain composure while brushing off the remnants of dead leaves from his jacket. 'What would you do in my situation?' he asked, seeking some semblance of camaraderie with the only ally he seemed to have at that moment.

Siegfried gave a dry chuckle. 'The same as you. I noticed you came back but said nothing. I guess rules can be flexible in emergencies,' he said with a smile.

With the ice broken, they stood side by side. Two figures united against a dangerous foe within the peaceful country-side that mocked their urgency. They quietly exchanged information, occasionally interrupted by the distant cooing of wood pigeons.

'Lister is cunning, and I now know he's armed. If my gut feeling is right, he'll do anything to get inside the hall,' Peter said, the officer nodding in agreement.

'Let's make sure of that,' the officer replied. 'We need to apprehend him as he enters the premises.'

Peter thought for a second or two. 'I know the answer to the question I'm about to ask, which is why I haven't raised it until now. However, I need to satisfy my curiosity. Why not pick up Lister now? You know, or at least you tell me you have him under direct observation. If that's the case, we can put this to bed now and remove the risk of my friends being harmed.'

Siegfried fixed Peter with an intense stare. All signs of comradery vanished. After what seemed like an age to Peter, his erstwhile companion answered. 'I'm under strict orders not to interfere in Lister's little adventure.'

Peter felt resentment and anger building. 'Little adventure? We're talking about people's lives here. How can you follow such an order?'

'Because we, too, inhabit quite different worlds. Do I have to spell it out to you, Peter?'

'What, whether an individual lives or dies being incidental to your mission?'

The officer continued to fix his gaze on Peter without answering the question.

Peter soon realised no answer would be forthcoming. At least he knew he'd been right when he postulated why Lister had escaped from the police station and allowed to roam the area unhindered. 'What a dirty world these people live in,' Peter thought.

At last, the intelligence officer broke his silence. 'Don't think too badly of us, Peter. Orders are one thing, but we won't let Lister hurt anyone if this lot goes to the wire.'

Saturday, 6th September 3.30 pm

PETER CROUCHED behind the gnarled trunk of an ancient oak, his heart pounding in rhythm with the distant thuds of cheery music that wafted from the hall. The officer, a silhouette against the twilight, acknowledged him with a sombre nod.

'Lister's not one to miss an opportunity,' Peter whispered, eyes darting through the foliage. 'He's going to try for the hall...it's where everyone is, vulnerable, distracted by everything that's going on.'

'Agreed,' the officer murmured, his voice barely audible. 'I'll have the team tighten the net around the building. And Allen—' he pressed a finger to his earpiece, 'keep your eyes on Lister. Don't blink, and for heaven's sake, stay hidden. Let me know the instant he makes for the building.'

Officers moved silently through the underbrush, forming an invisible shield around the celebrations. Peter felt a frisson of tension, knowing that the entire assembly may be in jeopardy.

'Updates, Allen,' the officer commanded softly, as if speaking to the spirits of the wood. A static crackle replied, affirming that Lister was still among the trees.

'Right, let's move.' The officer's hand gestured towards the hall, a sentinel guiding his charge. They slipped through the woods, feet treading lightly on the forest floor, leaving no trace but the whisper of their passing.

The officer's calm demeanour belied the urgency of their mission, his eyes sharp as flint beneath the brim of his cap. He paused. 'Positions,' he whispered into his concealed microphone. Like leaves caught in a gentle breeze, the officers closed in, unseen yet ever watchful.

———

Saturday, 6th September 5.15 pm

A RIPPLE of laughter undulated through the Great Hall as Fitch, resplendent in his haphazardly knotted tie, cleared his throat to command silence. He stood under the vaulted ceilings of the ancestral home, a mischievous glint dancing in his eyes. The guests leaned forward; anticipation tickling the air.

'Right,' he began, tapping the microphone which squawked in protest, 'You all know Anthony, our beloved groom, and local daredevil. But did you know about the time he tried to parachute from the vicarage roof...with nothing but a bedsheet?'

Chortles erupted around the room as Fitch painted a vivid tableau of youthful antics.

With each new anecdote, from Ant's infamous hedge-trimming disaster to his botched attempt at sheep shearing, Fitch wove a tapestry rich with the threads of his home. Guests shook their heads in mock despair and clinked glasses, celebrating the charming follies of the man of the hour.

Amid the gaiety, a sudden disruption tore through the convivial atmosphere. A series of sharp pops, like chestnuts on an open fire, echoed through the hall as smoke bombs discharged their disorienting haze. Instinctively, Peter's gaze snapped toward the entrance, his nerves taut as bowstrings.

Chaos bloomed amongst the revellers as wisps of smoke unfurled into billowing clouds, shrouding the grandeur of the hall in an opaque veil. The genteel murmurings turned to exclamations of alarm — wine glasses abandoned mid-toast.

From his vantage point, Peter caught a fleeting shadow slipping through the commotion—Lister. He moved as silent and cunning. His warning had come to fruition; the predator was amidst the flock.

'Ant!' Lyn's voice cut through the tumult, clear and authoritative despite the burgeoning pandemonium. Without hesitation, Ant's protective instincts surged. He wrapped Lyn in a shield of arms and resolve, ready to face whatever threat emerged from the encroaching fog.

'Stay down,' he murmured, his voice steady though his heart thundered like the hooves of wild Exmoor ponies. Lyn nodded, her own courage a beacon in the muddled gloom, her trust in Ant unwavering as they braced together amid the uncertainty.

The murmur of disturbed wildlife outside mirrored the unrest within. As a barn owl took flight, its white feathers ghostly against the darkening woods. Inside the hall, Peter meandered through the startled guests. He acted as a guardian in pursuit of justice, his focus unyielding despite the disarray.

'Everyone, please remain calm!' boomed the Earl's commanding tone, honed by years of military service. Yet even his presence couldn't dispel the edge of fear that laced the air, thick as the Norfolk mists that rolled in from the North Sea.

Fitch's speech lay forgotten, the echoes of laughter now replaced by the symphony of a mystery unfolding, as unpredictable and wild as the windswept landscapes of rural England.

The haze thickened, a woolly blanket of smoke that seemed to conspire with Lister's nefarious plans. Peter crouched low, squinting into the fog that swirled through the Great Hall like an unwanted guest. His heart galloped; each beat a drumroll in this farcical symphony of chaos.

'Left flank, by the tapestry. Move!' he rasped into the earpiece provided by an officer. Peter directed the officers through the muddle of coughing guests and overturned chairs. The wedding venue had turned into a battlefield, with canapes and champagne flutes as casualties strewn across the ornate carpet.

'Understood,' crackled the reply, nearly lost beneath the din of alarm.

Peter weaved through the crowd, a whisper of apologies and pardons forthcoming as he brushed past the ruffled finery of the guests. The air was a soup of confusion, flavoured with the distinct tang of fear and the faint scent of roses from Lyn's bouquet, now tragically abandoned on a table.

'Keep your eyes peeled,' Peter muttered, more to himself than anyone else.

As if the thickening smoke were slicing segments of time, each second became surreal. Disembodied voices rose and fell, the whirling waltz of panic rising to fever pitch. With the stealth of a countryside fox, Peter closed in, his gaze locking onto the shadowy figure of Lister inching closer to Ant and Lyn.

'Ant, down!' he shouted, but his voice was just another echo in the turmoil.

Lister, mere feet away from his targets, loomed like a storm cloud over a picnic. But before his darkness could rain down upon Ant and Lyn, Peter launched forward, his body springing into action like a coiled spring set loose.

The tackle was pure instinct, rugby honed on many a muddy field. They hit the ground with a thud that would have made the local badgers look up from their burrows in mild curiosity.

'Gotcha,' Peter grunted, fingers gripping Lister's jacket with the tenacity of ivy on an old stone wall.

Lister bucked and writhed, a dance of desperation under Peter's iron hold. They knocked over a table, upsetting a tower of champagne glasses which cascaded like a miniature waterfall.

'Stop, or I'll—' Peter's threat dissolved into a grunt as Lister's elbow found his ribs.

'Out of my way, you fool!' Lister snarled, clawing for any advantage.

Their struggle was a blur, limbs entangled, each man wrestling for dominance. It was less a ballet and more a country jig, with improvised steps, and toes inevitably trodden on.

From their protective cocoon, Ant and Lyn clung to each other, the commotion around them as jarring as a peacock's call shattering the morning stillness. Their breaths came in short bursts, hearts thundering louder than a winter storm.

'Come on, Peter,' Lyn whispered fiercely, her faith in the man unwavering as she gripped Ant's hand tighter.

And in the heart of the fray, amidst the roiling mist and clamour, Peter summoned every ounce of his country grit.

'Sorry, Lister,' he panted, delivering a final determined shove. 'This isn't your day.'

The scuffle between Peter and Lister had whipped the wedding reception into a swirling waltz of chaos. The Great Hall, once a setting for genteel celebrations, resembled a scene from an avant-garde play where the actors had forgotten their cues.

'Careful with the peonies!' came a cry as a vase toppled over, water seeping into the fabric of the ancient carpet.

'Watch the cake!' someone else shouted, though the confection was far from anyone's top priority at that moment.

Peter, his focus narrowed to the man beneath him, felt the tension in Lister's body coil like a spring. He pinned Lister's arm to the ground just as a deafening blast echoed through the hall, and time itself seemed to recoil in shock.

Screams cleaved the smoky air, rising and falling in a cacophony of terror and confusion.

'Who's hit? Who's shot?' the questions buzzed, but no answers came—only a thick silence that draped over the room like a shroud.

Peter held his breath, his ears ringing, his own heartbeat pounding a staccato rhythm against his ribcage as he searched for any sign of blood on his person. Nothing. He looked down at Lister, who lay grimacing beneath him. Blood oozed from his shoe.

'Blow me down. He's shot himself in the big toe,' Peter whispered. He wanted to laugh at the absurdity of it all.

'Everyone, please remain calm!' It was David, the butler, whose voice cut through the fog of panic employing the precision of a school bell ending dinner time. With efficiency, he strode across the room, flinging open windows and doors with the theatrics of a stage manager unveiling a set. Fresh air rushed in like an eager understudy, causing the smoke to retreat, revealing the aftermath of pandemonium.

'Ah, there it is,' David muttered, spotting the source of the gunshot wound.

Lister, now devoid of his previous menace, clutched his foot, his face contorted not with rage but with self-inflicted agony. The gun lay discarded nearby, a testament to the folly of haste.

'Mr. Lister shot himself in the foot, metaphorically and literally,' David announced with a dryness that would have made the Sahara jealous.

Lister groaned, wincing as he tried to sit up. His attempt at villainy had ended not with a bang, but with a whimper —and an ironic twist worthy of an Ealing comedy.

'Didn't your mother ever tell you to be careful with firearms?' Peter quipped, drawing a few relieved chuckles from the gathering crowd. They had been prepared for a showdown, perhaps even a tragedy, but certainly not for this slapstick conclusion.

'Should've stuck to knitting socks in prison, old boy,' one of the intelligence officers added. A ripple of laughter followed.

As the last tendrils of smoke drifted out into the Norfolk countryside, the guests' fear melted into murmurs of disbelief and gratitude. The wedding, despite its dramatic interruption, was still a day for celebration. Lister may have grabbed attention briefly, but the genuine heroes were Peter, Fitch—the clever groomsman, and David, the calm butler.

Peter retrieved the gun from the floor and emptied the chamber as if he'd just come off a practice firing range.

The wedding guests, had moments ago, had clapped along to Fitch's tales of Ant's less-than-stellar dance moves. Now they formed a semi-circle of wide-eyed curiosity. Phyllis caught everyone's attention with a bird decoration that had fallen from her hat and perched on her shoulder. She looked like a pirate who'd misplaced their ship and visited a wrestling match instead.

'Quite the spectacle, isn't it, Betty?' Phyllis remarked, not so quietly. The bird bobbed its head as if in agreement.

'Indeed, Phyllis,' Betty murmured, her words nearly lost beneath her friend's more robust commentary.

The smoke, now only a light mist clinging to the ground, danced lazily in the beams of sunlight streaming through the newly opened windows. As visibility returned, David stepped forward, his voice cutting through the remaining tension with the ease of a seasoned diplomat.

'My Lords, ladies, and gentlemen. If I may have your attention,' he began, a smile touching his lips. 'Kindly make your way to the Grand Gallery for refreshments. The bride and groom will shortly grace us with their first dance.'

A collective sigh, part relief, and part delight, rippled through the crowd, followed by applause. Some guests were already chattering excitedly about the turn of events they'd witnessed.

'Never a dull moment in Norfolk,' Peter said to himself, watching the guests filter out with a shake of his head. He couldn't help but agree with David's subtle implication—the day would indeed go on, and so too would the stories of the wedding that a rogue had almost upstaged. An escaped prisoner and his inability to shoot straight.

The detective's arms, still tingling with the adrenaline from the confrontation, now wrapped themselves around Lyn and Ant in a protective embrace. The chaos had ebbed away like the tide leaving the Norfolk beaches. In its stead bloomed a palpable sense of tranquillity that seemed to sizzle through their interlocked bodies.

'Is everyone alright?' Lyn asked, her voice steady despite the whirlwind they'd just endured. Her once perfectly styled blond hair now showed signs of the day's unexpected events, with a few strands sticking to her lipstick.

'Couldn't be better,' Ant quipped, his words and tone a testament to understatement. There was a look in his eye that mirrored the smile curling at the edge of Peter's mouth.

'Except for maybe Lister,' Peter added, glancing over his shoulder at the immobilised culprit being led away, big toe still smarting from his self-inflicted injury.

They remained stationary a moment longer. The trio at the heart of the storm that had blown through their lives now dissipated as quickly as it arrived. Birds chirped outside, indifferent to the human drama, their songs a soundtrack to the renewal of calm.

'Shall we then?' Lyn gestured towards the Grand Gallery where the laughter and clinking of glasses promised a return to festivities.

'Absolutely,' Peter said, releasing them both from the hug but catching Lyn's hand, holding onto the connection a moment longer. 'After all, we can't let a little thing like a would-be killer ruin a good party.'

'Norfolk's reputation for excitement remains undiminished,' Ant proclaimed. To emphasise the point, he led the way with a mock-heroic stride.

As they moved towards the gallery, the landscape beyond the windows beckoned, its timeless beauty undisturbed by the brief intrusion of danger.

'Race you to the champagne?' Lyn proposed.

'Wouldn't dream of it,' Ant teased, matching her stride. 'After today, I think we all deserve a victory lap.'

Peter watched on as the newlyweds tore up the yards on their quest to be first to the champagne. Just as he began moving forward to join the celebratory throng, a hand on his shoulder rooted the detective to the spot.

'Don't worry,' began a familiar voice. 'No more fighting today.'

Peter turned to see Siegfried smiling. 'That's the second time you've done that to me today. Why can't you announce yourself like any ordinary human being?' He tried to hold a stern posture. However, the relief of the afternoon ending in success go the better of him as returned his new friend's greeting.

'And that's the thanks I get for keeping my promise to tell you why we let Lister loose after we nicked him from your, eh,…nick'

'Oh, very droll,' replied the happy detective. Gone on, then. I'm all ears.'

As the two professionals strolled towards a staff member carrying a tray of drinks, Siegfried leaned into Peter. 'We had a tip off that someone we had an interest in had caught wind of Lister's whereabouts. My boss wanted this little rabbit to run. You see, the person in question was a gentleman...and I use that word lightly, who we'd been after for some time. Let's just say he held a treasure trove of information His Majesty's government remains keen to get its hands on.

'Nope, still don't get it,' whispered Peter.

'You make things hard, don't you?' Siegfried replied. 'The only other thing I can tell you is that Lister wasn't the only one who wanted revenge.'

'Ah, now I get it. You intended to use Lister as bait? Did he turn up?

'Not this time, but we'll get him in due course.'

'What a warped world you guys occupy,' Peter teased.

Siegfried smiled again. 'Let's just say we live in a parallel world, just as the police do. After all, it wouldn't do for the public to realise what kind of world they're actually living in, now would it?'

As the band struck up with the first tune of the afternoon, Ant, and Lyn took to the dance floor for their first dance as a married couple, the two men, both intelligence officers in their own way, clinked their lead-crystal glasses together.

'To a job well done,' said Siegfried with an enigmatic edge to his voice.

Epilogue

Saturday, 6th September 9.00 pm

AS THE SUN dipped below the horizon, it cast a warm glow over the Stanton's grand home. The once bustling Great Hall now stood silent, its walls echoing memories of laughter, vows, and celebration. Today's wedding had been a resounding success, a testament to love and tradition.

Lyn and Ant, now officially husband and wife, stood hand in hand on the threshold of their new life. The oak banisters, once adorned with pastel ribbons, bore witness to their union. The fairy lights that had tangled in Ant's hands during the preparations now twinkled softly, illuminating the path ahead.

The Earl and Countess Stanton, still resplendent in their morning suits and silver-white hair, watched from a distance. Their eyes held a mixture of pride and nostalgia. Countess Stanton had become 'Mum' to Lyn, and the earl revelled in the role of 'Dad.' Their little slice of history had expanded to include a new chapter—one filled with promise and hope.

And then there was Peter. An unassuming figure, he had been their confidant and collaborator on countless investigations. His salt-and-pepper hair and perpetually furrowed brow spoke of a man who had seen both the best and worst of humanity. He stood slightly apart, observing the scene with a detective's keen eye.

As the wind rustled the leaves outside, Lyn leaned into Ant's embrace. 'We've done it,' she whispered. 'We're married.'

Ant chuckled, his eyes reflecting the same wonder. 'Our own slice of tradition,' he said. 'And a love that stands the test of time.'

The countess approached, her steps graceful as ever. 'Traditions are like old oaks,' she said in a wise tone. 'They endure storms, get stronger each season, and protect generations.'

Her husband nodded in agreement. 'And love,' he added, 'is the heartwood that binds it all together.'

Peter cleared his throat, stepping forward. His trench coat hung loosely around his frame, and the lines etched on his face told stories of mysteries solved and justice served. 'Well,' he said, his gruff voice softening, 'I've seen my fair share of weddings and crime scenes, but this one—' He gestured toward the newlyweds. 'This one's special.'

Lyn smiled at him. 'Peter, you've been our rock,' she said. 'The one who unravelled the knots when everything seemed impossible.'

Ant nodded. 'Our friend and partner,' he said. 'Always there, even when the clues led us down dark alleys.'

Peter's eyes crinkled at the corners. 'Just doing my job,' he mumbled, but there was warmth in his gaze.

And so, as the stars emerged in the darkening sky, the newlyweds stepped forward into their future. The fragrance of peonies lingered, a sweet reminder of beginnings. The Great Hall, now empty, held the echoes of their laughter and promises, as well as the unspoken gratitude for Peter's unwavering presence.

As for Fitch, the longtime friend who had shared countless pints at the Wherry Arms, he raised an imaginary glass from afar. 'To Lyn, Ant, and Peter,' he murmured, 'may their love be as enduring as Stanton Hall itself.'

And so it was. A love woven into the fabric of tradition. A promise whispered by the wind, and an epilogue written in the language of the heart, with Peter and Fitch's name etched alongside theirs.

More by Keith Finney

vinci-books.com/poshmurder

High tea, high society, and high stakes...

When the Dowager Duchess of Drakeford stumbles upon a corpse during a manor picnic, her sleuthing instincts spring to life in this charming 1920s whodunit. Summoning her butler, Rex Sutherland, and Scotland Yard's Inspector Whipple, the clever Dowager navigates love triangles, bitter rivalries, and scandalous secrets among the sophisticated suspects.

Turn the page for a free preview...

A Posh Murder: Chapter One

QUITE A PICNIC

'Are you certain the gentleman is dead, Rex? Perhaps he merely sleeps, albeit in a peculiar position.'

There was no escaping the fact. Before us lay the prone body of a man, I took to be a little older than my twenty-one years. His unnatural position, face down over the immense girth of a fallen tree by a beautiful lake, legs akimbo and left arm outstretched, gave the gentleman – for that's what he appeared to be from the quality of his attire – the look of someone who had attempted to simulate the breaststroke with disastrous consequences.

I noted two curious facts: the surprised expression on his motionless face, and the second, that his left hand rested palm-upward with his index and middle finger elegantly extended in the manner of a thespian acting out his tragic demise.

I recounted these facts to my employer, Eleanor, Dowager Duchess of Drakeford, an amateur sleuth of great repute in certain circles.

'Many people who meet their end suddenly, bear the

countenance of yonder fellow. It is because the individual thinks to themselves, "So this is what it feels like", or exhibits utter surprise that an acquaintance is about to do them in, so to speak.'

Before I had time to gather my thoughts, HG asked that I nip back to the Rolls to recover a heavy wool blanket. At first, I thought it might be to cover the deceased gentlemen out of respect. Not so. My Lady bade me lay the hand-knitted Shetland weave on a bare patch of soil by the water's edge, whereupon she'd inadvertently disturbed a colony of red ants. The blanket proved a perfect antidote to their shenanigans as HG tucked into her favourite sand-wiches: smoked salmon with a hint of Fortnum and Mason special relish and sea-salt sent from the Outer Hebrides on annual consignment.

'Do you think the gentleman has been here long?' I asked.

Without breaking stride from sipping her specially mixed Twinings English Afternoon Tea blend, HG esti-mated his final decline as being one hour, fifty-seven minutes earlier. When I enquired about the precise nature of her calculation, HG remarked the man's frozen facial features and rigid hand bore all the hallmarks of rigor mortis having recently set in.

Rigor mortis was a revelation to me. Although having reached my majority the previous month, the only dead body I'd hitherto observed was that of my Uncle Cedric, who had died of a troublesome liver and was secured into his coffin in what I thought indecent haste.

His wake at the Dog and Duck was a splendid event, though it was later said the owner fell into a rapid decline, as did his profits, once Uncle Cedric ceased favouring the establishment with his business.

Having replenished HG's tea and arranged the dainty cakes on a silver platter to her liking, I inspected the unfortunate gentleman. I gazed in wonder that not a hair on his head was out of place, save for a gaping wound along his neat centre parting. Yet I saw not the faintest of marks upon his hands.

'It seems to me, HG, that he failed to put up any resistance to the violent onslaught. Odd, don't you think, when someone is intent on bumping you off?'

The dowager took some persuading to put down her iced fancy and entertain my deduction. However, dispatched to the Rolls-Royce for a replacement fancy, I returned to observe the dowager getting to her feet quite energetically for a woman of advancing years with a clicky hip.

I now witnessed the master at work. Disturbed from her recreational pursuits, HG circled the body like a ravenous lion stalking its prey.

She gesticulated as if bashing someone over the head by raising her hand and allowing it to descend violently. Alas, this caused HG's iced fancy to fly from her iron grip and hit the unfortunate fellow square on the left temple. 'I had been enjoying that,' she remarked.

Reaching into the inside pocket of the fellow's jacket, HG withdrew an expensive-looking leather wallet and opened it. 'His name is Ambrose Bagley,' she said, inspecting his motor vehicle driving licence. 'Born April 1899, so he was twenty-three. He lived at a good address in Knightsbridge, I notice.'

As she methodically sifted through each compartment, two five-pound notes came to light, as well as four one penny red postage stamps and a folded newspaper cutting.

'How curious.' The dowager handed me the sliver of

paper. One side contained an advertisement for 'Blenkin's Elixir, sure to keep you moving', which I presumed was not pertinent to the matter at hand. On the other, among a short list of announcements, one stood out with two short, heavy lines having been drawn in the margin. The advert read:

Will you at ten? W. Halt

In the final compartment, HG recovered a ticket stub. It pointed to a train journey from London Charing Cross terminating locally. In tiny writing in one corner, someone, presumably the deceased, had scribbled 'Arrive 10.42 am'.

'I estimate the walk from the station to this location took him not more than fifteen minutes. Given it's now one thirty by the church clock and we found the fellow not ten minutes since, he cannot have croaked it before 11.07 am. It is clear to me he won't recover. In fact, I doubt he knew what hit him, although I'm sure he knew precisely who finished him. Your excellent and most astute observation tells me this chap made no attempt to fend off his attacker.'

I marvelled at the skill and diligence that HG devoted to the stranger. After all, we could have simply packed our things away and returned to Drakeford, seat of the dowager's deceased husband's family since 1216. Not to put too fine a point on matters. The stranger was as dead as it was possible to be, so no further harm could befall him.

However, that was not how HG saw things. As she was often to remind me over the years, her motto remained *invenire omnes*: 'to find out all', or FOA as she preferred to say.

Surveying the sombre scene, HG instructed we should repair to our host for the weekend, Colonel Crispen Percival-Travers (Retired) at Bircham Manor, in whose extensive grounds we happened upon the tragic Ambrose.

'Do hurry, Rex, or we shall be late. Crispen does a wonderful lunch. It's absolutely famed throughout the Home Counties.'

My instructions clear, I secured the wicker picnic basket on the running board of the Rolls, ensured the dowager remained comfortably seated in the limousine's rear and rejoined the mile-and-a-half of newly laid gravel drive that led to the front entrance of the Manor.

'Make haste, Rex; we must advise the colonel of our discovery and insist he call for Whipple of Scotland Yard at once.'

———

Several well-turned-out ladies and gentlemen milled around the front entrance as the house staff removed luggage from a variety of fine vehicles. Of these, one or two appeared to disturb HG's otherwise calm countenance.

'I see he's invited the Watkins-Simms twins. Mark my words; sparks, not to say fisticuffs, shall fly before the weekend is over.'

HG pointed to the younger twin and his wife, who I thought was an unusual match. The husband was a small chap with a balding crown, his dignity preserved by a severe comb-over topping a sombre day suit and Oxford shoes. The man twitched from time to time when his wife offered an icy stare.

Although they appeared to be a similar age, which I estimated to be the wrong side of fifty, the lady wore an ensemble reminiscent of the young ladies known as 'flappers', a point not lost on two such girls pointing and giggling from the safety of a dashing Bentley, which looked resplendent in its livery of British Racing Green.

The elder of the Watkins-Simms, on the other hand, appeared sporty and full of the joys of spring in their matching tennis whites and swinging their rackets with such gusto that the wife almost clipped a footman removing crocodile skin weekend cases from their Citroen motor vehicle.

'Those two hate each other. Twin brothers, would you believe? I've tried several times to effect a reconciliation, but the soberly dressed one, and eleven minutes the younger, refuses all efforts. Still, what can you do when, for the sake of the time it takes to prepare and cook a couple of good omelettes, the elder inherits their father's considerable estate?'

I thought the cooking analogy was a funny one for HG to choose, since she once confided in me that the nearest she'd come to cooking was heating a kettle on the great range of Drakeford Hall. All appeared well, she recounted, until a hissing sound became apparent and on inspection, so insufficient was the water in the brass kettle to sustain being heated that a hole appeared in its substantial base.

'We must find the colonel. There isn't a second to lose,' announced HG as she neglected to wait for me to open the car door for her, instead launching herself forth so that two nearby footmen almost bumped heads when bowing, so flustered were they at the dowager's rapid progress through the open front doors to the Manor house.

Wasting no time in following my employer, Lomas, the butler, did all in his power to bar my entry to the grand house. 'To the kitchen door, my man,' he said in a lofty tone.

Fortunately, HG remained within hearing range of the remark and educated the aged, and I thought, slightly tipsy, butler. 'Rex is my man. In fact, he is my Man of all Works, and must attend me.'

Lomas clearly took the dowager's remark with disdain as he elevated his head and gave the air an exaggerated sniff.

'Am I understood?' insisted HG.

'As you wish, Your Grace,' came the surly reply as he shifted half a pace to his right and eyed me from head to foot as I passed into the Jacobean entrance hall, resplendent with a grand ebonised oak staircase and panelling, soot-scarred from a large open fire.

'What kind of job title is that, Eleanor?' The booming voice of the colonel filled the vast space as a rotund elderly gentleman in a pair of plus fours and Norfolk shooting jacket bounded down the wide stairs with such gusto that his complexion bore a distinctly purple hue by the time he kissed My Lady on both cheeks and pointed a gnarled forefinger at me.

Two worldly wise Irish wolfhounds bolted for the great hall as the colonel stepped across the stone-paved reception area to give me a closer inspection. HG said later this was because they thought the colonel's appearance meant exercise, something she gathered they preferred not to partake in.

'Man of all Works, you say?' The colonel strode purposefully over to me and did a turn about my person, as if inspecting a new beast for his famous herd of Aberdeen Angus cattle. 'Does he cook? I've heard that some of the smaller households of the middling sort employ a *Maid* of all Works. That is, a single female servant to run the house. Never a man.'

HG set about her host. 'Well, since my eldest son inherited the estate, I live in modest accommodation.'

The colonel continued to press his logic. 'Eleanor, I

understand you have two gardeners, a cook and a kitchen assistant, plus many other house staff. Hardly a small entourage, I think?'

The dowager dismissed his claim with a flick of her gloved hand and bade the butler furnish her with a telephone. 'Rex tends to my needs when away from the house, so you shall see him in various states of attire so as not to disturb the senseless sensibilities of your other guests.' She gave the colonel no opportunity to seek further clarification before continuing her forceful narration. 'Listen to me, Crispen; Rex and I have found a deceased person on your land and you must allow me to ring Scotland Yard forthwith. Where is that telephone?'

The colonel's face was a picture as he hurried toward the butler, whose scowl seemed permanent, to comply with the dowager's request, while trying to make sense of the disturbing information.

'A deceased person, you say. Do we know him?'

HG shook her head. 'It is one Ambrose Bagley of Knightsbridge. I once knew a Bagshot who disgraced himself in front of Her Majesty, Queen Victoria, but Bagley? I think not.'

Colonel Percival-Travers appeared nonplussed. 'No, can't say I know the family, either. I wonder what he was doing on my land. Too much trespassing nowadays, if you ask me.'

Just then, his wife, Augustine, breezed into the hall carrying an elegant vase full of deep red roses, smelling their scent as she glided across the stone floor. 'Don't be so silly, darling. Of course we know the Bagleys. They stayed with us during Wimbledon. Don't you remember, the boy has an excellent backhand.'

'Not now he hasn't,' replied the colonel, which I thought was in poor taste.

'Why ever not, Crispen; is he injured?'

I attempted to catch the dowager's attention, except she was too busy supervising the now cowering butler in placing the telephone at a comfortable height to save HG's clicky hip from playing up.

'Do you never listen, my darling? The boy isn't injured; he's bally-well dead. Eleanor is, as we speak, in conference with Whipple of the Yard.' The colonel pointed to the dowager as she dismissed the butler with a flea in his ear.

'Where did you get him from, for heaven's sake, Augustine?'

The colonel's wife sighed at HG and waved her free hand as if wishing the problem might go away. 'I know, Eleanor, but good staff are difficult to find nowadays. However, on the plus side, he's jolly good at banging the dinner gong on time, so at least we eat hot food these days. Anyway, I have much to do if we are to be ready for all our guests. Please give my regards to Mr Whipple-Yard, though I have to say I consider it a strange name.'

———

By the time I collected Inspector Whipple and his two constables from the station, deposited them at the Manor, changed into my day suit and entered the orangery, after-noon tea had already begun.

'Haven't I met you before? You look familiar. Have I nicked you for anything?' asked Whipple with a certain sharpness to his voice as I progressed through the glass and cast-iron marvel, collected a plate and transited several sandwich and cake stands to fulfil HG's catering needs.

I gave a polite bow from the neck and explained I had recently delivered him from the train station.

'And now you eat cucumber sandwiches and Victoria sponge with your betters. How extraordinary.'

Used to such a reaction in the short time I'd enjoyed the dowager's patronage, I continued about my business.

'Her Grace calls him her Man of all Works,' explained the colonel before asking Whipple if he wished to divest himself of his heavy overcoat and trilby, if only to avert heatstroke in the humid atmosphere of the glazed construction.

He refused the colonel's suggestion and, instead, continued to sweat profusely, leaving a trail of sweat droplets from his glistening nose on the red-tiled floor as he moved around.

Several minutes later, Whipple called the assembly to order. As he did so, one of the Irish wolfhounds dragged a silver server containing Coleman's mustard under the table behind the police officer.

'My name is Whipple; Whipple of the Yard.'

As I monitored the wolfhound, I glimpsed the colonel's wife straining to speak.

'Of which yard? Do we know such a place, my dear?' The colonel tried to ignore his wife.

'No, no, madam. *Scotland* Yard. In short, I am Chief Inspector Whipple of Scotland Yard.'

As Augustine and Whipple continued to confuse one another, I detected the wolfhound's unease as he finished the last of the mustard. The animal made strange noises from both ends of its impressive torso.

I could see HG had detected the dog's strange murmurings and increasingly agitated body movements. The dowager's efforts to interject the conversation between two people clearly misunderstanding each other's position failed, so the inevitable happened.

The hound issued forth at both ends, yelped, and ran for the duck pond.

'Has someone died?' said Augustine, such was the smell that even the citrus fruit failed to disguise.

I noted HG had seen and heard enough. 'Someone *has* died, and I suggest, Inspector Whipple, that you, Rex and I proceed to the crime scene at pace.'

A Posh Murder: Chapter Two

AN ANNOUNCEMENT

Ambrose Bagley remained much as we'd left him earlier in the day, except the phenomenon of rigor mortis now held the fellow in its tight grip.

In fact, the deceased might easily have been mistaken for an ironing board were it not for his brogue shoes, to which the dowager objected, because a gentleman would never consider such a vulgar shade of tan.

Inspector Whipple assumed command of the crime scene as if marshalling his troops ready for action. First, he ordered his two constables to scour the immediate area for anything that might imply a connection to the victim. Then he asked HG to recount our finding of Ambrose.

It immediately struck me as surprising how well they got on. The dowager was dazzling in an almost luminescent green three-quarter pleated skirt in the latest fashion with a light jacket and snug-fitting cloche hat. HG's ensemble favoured sensible day shoes with sturdy Louis heels.

For Whipple's part, he continued to sweat in his light brown mackintosh raincoat and a dark brown trilby. For a plainclothes policeman, his attire did not strike me as offering a high degree of anonymity. His tall frame and pale pallor gave the impression of a man suffering from seasickness, rather than the strong bearing one might expect of Scotland Yard's world-famous crime-solver.

'The sight of blood and corpses doesn't agree with the inspector's constitution,' HG later confided, which I thought bizarre, given his line of business.

At any rate, the pair got on like a house on fire, with each challenging the other's view with close attention and respect.

'You see, the poor fellow's expression? As if surprised and disappointed at the same time.'

Whipple rubbed his clean-shaven chin between a finger and thumb as he leaned forward to test HG's assessment. 'Then you're suggesting the man knew his assailant? As for his disappointment, I think that is natural given the outcome of what took place here.'

I pondered Whipple's latter point. So far, discussion surrounded the nature of Ambrose's position and injuries and not how or why he came to be beside the lake. I put this point to him, who at first gave me a suspicious look.

'Are you sure I haven't nicked you for something recently? A burglary perhaps, or the taking of a motor vehicle?'

Thankfully, HG put a stop to his interrogation. 'Cease this silliness, Arthur. You know perfectly well that Rex conveyed you from the train station. That he now wears a day suit instead of a chauffeur's uniform does not disguise the fact that it's the same fellow.'

The inspector looked me up and down, peering at me through almost closed eyes. 'Rex – what sort of name is that for a chap?'

I looked to HG for further support on the matter.

'It is enough for you to know I consider this young man as my apprentice. I'm tutoring him in the art of sleuthing, speaking of which, I take it we agree the murderer knew Ambrose Bagley?'

The dowager's explanation of my status immediately changed Whipple's countenance toward me. Instead of taking an unhealthy interest in the possibility I was a criminal, the man merely sniffed the air and ignored my presence after offering a final half-glance and a sort of sucking sound.

'Yes, I'm satisfied the assailant knew his victim and given you and several others are here for the weekend, I think it is safe to say that our murderer lurks among the colonel's houseguests.'

I suggested he gather everyone in the great hall to interview them one by one.

'I am not an invention of Agatha Christie's imagination a la Hercule Poirot, sir. I'm engaged in an official Scotland Yard investigation as opposed to an instalment in the *Weekly Times*.'

'Stop this at once, Whipple. Again, you play the fool for reasons I cannot fathom. As for his suggestion, I think it is quite an innovation.'

Whipple glanced in my direction before commenting, 'Quite so, HG.'

Fascinated that the dowager allowed the chief inspector to address her as HG, I observed the exchanges between a Scotland Yard thief-taker at the height of his powers and an aristocrat with an impeccable lineage, and the connection would continue to puzzle me for some time to come. For the time being, I settled for listening to HG persuade Whipple to adopt my strategy.

However, there was to be one more surprise as we left

Ambrose to the care of the medical profession. HG asked Whipple if he had the time. The inspector instinctively reached for his fob watch, tucked into a small pocket in his waistcoat and secured with a silver chain.

'Getting on for five o'clock.'

'Precisely as I thought,' replied HG, though I did not at first appreciate the significance of her enquiry. 'Let me ask you a question, Arthur. Do you know of any man worth his salt who does not own a fob watch?'

I clandestinely checked my own to confirm ownership as Whipple harrumphed. 'In my experience, men who do not own a fob watch are of the dubious sort and inherently untrustworthy.'

HG clapped her hands as she gazed at the corpse. 'Are we to conclude that the fellow is a bounder, then?'

Drawn to the deceased's garish waistcoat, which was plain to see now the chap was as stiff as a board, I deduced the meaning of HG's enquiry. Ambrose wore no such accessory.

Whipple eyed this latest revelation with interest. 'Perhaps that's why he holds his left hand thus, as if reaching out to recover something. Perhaps the killer removed the fob watch without this fellow's permission. What an unpleasant fellow the culprit must be.'

'I agree, Arthur.' As my ward suggested, we must now gather the assembly and put method into our investigations.'

———

The great hall of Bircham Manor was, like much of the Manor, remodelled in the 1870s in the Neo-Gothic style. One might say the building served as a testimony to

Augustus Welby Pugin, who could have been accused of getting carried away when he designed the interior of our noble Houses of Parliament.

Gone were any traces of Tudor magnificence or the gaiety of dainty Georgian colour schemes. Now all was heavy burgundies and stained oak furniture, which gave the voluminous room more the look of a court room than state room. However, this fitted our bill perfectly as a procession of staff entered the room from one end and the gentry from the opposite elevation.

I stood to one side as Chief Inspector Whipple and the dowager took centre stage. In front of them sat two rows of chairs, adjacent but with a gap between them in the manner of church pews. Staff to the left and gentry to the right.

'I have summoned you here to begin my investigations into the heinous murder of one Ambrose Bagley, late of Knightsbridge and, I suspect, a guest in this grand house for the weekend.' Whipple cast his arms about as if emphasising the immenseness of the Manor.

A hand shot up from the midst of the servant section. 'That is correct, Inspector. The gentleman was to stay in the Chinese bedroom, although I don't suppose he'll need it now, will he?'

The dowager entered the fray. 'Is this the case, Colonel?'

I thought it weird that the retired military gentleman appeared not to be familiar with his guests for the weekend.

'I expect my son, Peregrine, asked the chap. You know what these young fellows are like.'

A pause ensued as the assembly waited for said son to respond. 'Oh, he's not here,' said the colonel. 'he'll be pressing flowers or whatever it is would-be botanists get up to.'

I noted Whipple shook his head, which I took as a

measure of the famed inspector's frustration at the slow pace of progress.

'Let me be clear with you all. My view is that the person who murdered Ambrose Bagley is in this room or pressing flowers.' A tidal wave of murmurs coursed along the rows of people present. 'In which case, no one is to leave the house or grounds without my express consent. Is that understood?' The inspector's eagle eye cast its predatory stare from one to the next, defying dissent of any sort.

The quiet sob of a female floated from the back of the room. At the doorway to the great room leaned Rowena Dosett, a well-known flapper who kept rooms at the Ritz Hotel. The small, slim lady, dressed in a pastel blue frock and matching Mary Jane pumps, dabbed her eyes with a lace handkerchief.

'Did you know the deceased, miss?'

Whipple's directness caused HG to gravitate toward the young woman, who failed to answer the chief inspector's question.

Fed up with waiting, Whipple dismissed all present by repeating his order that no one should leave the premises and that they should each expect an interview on the matter.

'I'll leave you to consider two matters,' he concluded. 'If you're the guilty party, it's in your own best interest that you come forward, for I shall find the culprit. Make no mistake about that. Second, should you have any information about the murder, heard or saw anything you think might interest the police, then it's your duty in upholding His Majesty's peace that you speak to me confidentially.'

Shortly after, Whipple began interviewing the paid staff while the houseguests and their host retired to the morning room for tea and crumpets.

Such gatherings provided me with an astonishing insight into how HG went about her sleuthing. As I occupied myself with examining a portfolio of pressed flowers compiled by the colonel's son in a bay window seat of the delightfully presented morning room, the dowager directed the conversation in such a way as to benefit her investigation while doing nothing to undermine her great friend Arthur Whipple.

Although I was unable to hear all the conversation, the titbits I picked up, together with HG telling me all later, propelled our investigations into unchartered territory.

I here recall a flavour of the dowager's technique to elicit information of import.

Sitting close by Rowena Dosett, HG attempted to comfort the young lady. 'Did you know Ambrose well?' This was a term the dowager always deployed to great effect. Although spoken with a true heart and natural integrity, it did the trick in disarming the beneficiary.

'I loved him dearly, and we were engaged.'

The announcement brought a gasp from one section of the room and derision from others.

'Why do you mock, young sir? You're Berty Blowers' sole offspring, are you not?' His lack of response did not go down well with HG. 'Speak, boy. Are you related to that rascal of a man or are you not? Come, speak up, man.'

The man smirked. 'I have that pleasure, Your Grace. And I did not smirk, at least not at the young lady. Ambrose deserves no better than he got. The man was a bounder and a cad.'

'Fredrick Blowers, you have no right to talk about my Ambrose like that. He was a perfect gentleman and particularly good at playing the saxophone, which I'm told is a most difficult instrument to master. What have you to show for your life to date? A failed Bolivian gold mine venture through which you ruined several perfectly respectable gentlemen, and an abiding habit of grinding your teeth?'

I noted the gentleman immediately stopped moving his lower jaw from side to side, which led me to believe he took Miss Dosett's accusation to heart. Perhaps the fellow wasn't so jaunty after all.

Unexpectedly, a second gentleman sallied forth. 'Ambrose was a decent sort, but not good enough for you, my darling Rowena.' The chap's protestation looked even stranger given the white trousers, pink and white striped boating blazer, and straw boater which, for some inexplicable reason, he failed to remove while indoors.

Miss Dosett's response paved the way for several additional avenues HG and I were to follow in pursuit of Ambrose's murderer. 'Dear Lemuel, I love you as a brother, but nothing more. We have talked about this so often since being presented at court. It is simply not to be, my loyal friend.'

'Then I shall kill myself, just as I...' But the man tailed off with a faraway look.

After the tense atmosphere of the morning room, HG and I enjoyed a pleasant walk in the extensive grounds of the Manor. From our vantage point, we could see house staff coming and going from the great hall as Whipple continued interviewing all persons on the premises.

'Are we to believe that young Lemuel Norris accosted Ambrose and we are, in fact, investigating a crime of passion?'

At first, I found the proposition attractive, but considered it too convenient that a young man should make a statement tantamount to an admission of murder. I expressed my concerns to HG, who appeared to be busy watching one of the ground staff.

'We should talk to the gardener. If in the grounds this morning, he may have heard or seen something.' By 'we,' I knew HG meant me and made a mental note of the task. 'Now, we were discussing Lemuel, were we not? I suppose you may have a point that it's too convenient. Another way of looking at this is that the boy intentionally made himself look silly and, therefore, harmless when, in fact, he's our murderer. I call such people clever fools. It plays to their hand to be thought imbecilic. It allows them the time and space to complete whatever it is they're up to.'

I reflected on this point. Eventually concluding such an approach may lead one to jump at one's own shadow in attempting to untangle real from imagined conspiracies.

Our deliberations ceased as Whipple appeared on the horizon. HG commented he looked like a man needing a friend, so we doubled back to greet him. His mood appeared dark as he removed his trilby and wiped a layer of perspiration from his brow.

'If one more person informs me what a nice place, the Manor is to work, and how kind the family is to their staff, I shall puke.'

HG questioned why he should see anything but truth in the matter.

Inspector Whipple said that if something sounds too good to be true, then it usually is too good to be true. He added that, 'No family is perfect, for this is how the Percival-Travers are being portrayed, and I don't buy it.'

The dowager held her counsel, which I at first thought strange, since HG was not a woman to hold back when something needed saying or doing. Eventually, she ceased opening and closing her parasol as a measure to abate midges and stuck the steel tip into the soft ground as if about to use it as a shooting stick. 'Far be it from me to cast aspersions. However, I understand young Peregrine likes to press more than flowers. In fact, he has quite a reputation for visiting the ladies in certain noble homes in our capital city.'

HG had given me another valuable lesson in her many skills as a sleuth of repute. Born in 1856, Her Grace, or the Honourable Miss Eleanor Fitzgibbons as she was then, grew up among the very highest of society and named Queen Victoria as a godmother figure. In later years, the queen retained HG as a close confidant. This position, combined with a good marriage, maintained that HG was able to open any door she wished to enter.

The dowager informs me she still enjoys extensive access to the very highest circles, after going through a rough patch between 1901 and 1910 when Queen Victoria's eldest son, Bertie, was king. 'A man of eccentric morals who had an even more eccentric chair-like construction made for him in Paris', was all she said on the matter.

However, HG conceded his great triumph in establishing the Entente Cordiale with the French in 1904, when relations soured between our two countries. 'He went to Paris with them virtually throwing rocks at him and came away a couple of weeks later with the French eating out of his hands.'

As I mused on the matter, I lost sight of HG and Whipple. Only the inspector's distinct growl alerted me to their location as he berated one of his constables for not being correctly turned out as a member of His Majesty's constabulary.

'Adjust your article, PC Willows, or you'll be walking in front of the commissioner's car with a red flag.'

I arrived in time to observe the hapless bobby repositioning the strap on his helmet, so it rested on the cusp of, rather than under, his chin. Foolishly, I thought, the constable, who I took to be around my age, contested the matter.

'But sir, parliament repealed the Locomotive Act in 1896. The law no longer exists.'

Over the many years, I would collaborate with Whipple. What followed was one of only perhaps three occasions I witnessed the inspector almost resort to physical violence.

'Young man,' started the inspector ominously, 'I am the law. If I say you'll walk in the road carrying a red flag before you, that's what you'll do. Do not think for one moment that your knowledge of the law impresses me. Showing off isn't something I admire in my officers. In fact, knowing too much may positively harm your career. So that you may reflect on matters, you'll now scout the entire estate for further evidence and report to me when completed. Now get out of my sight.'

'But sir, the cook says tea will be ready in an hour.'

'Then you'd better get a move on. Jenkins, you get back to the Manor house and see what you can dig up from the younger servants.'

Though I felt sympathy for PC Willows, I couldn't help feeling he'd brought the wrath of Scotland Yard down on his own head. Conversely, PC Jenkins appeared pleased with the turn of events.

HG had waited patiently throughout the episode, something I took as a measure of her respect for the inspector. However, now she appeared restless. 'Let us get on. We must isolate the houseguests from one another and capture their recollection of events and their views of poor Ambrose.'

Entering the front door to the Manor while ignoring the crotchety butler, we were presented with a scene of mayhem before us. Rushing down the grand staircase came Rowena Dosett in floods of tears, followed quickly by Lemuel Norris.

'What a terrible thing for you to say,' wailed the inconsolable Rowena.

'What did he say, I wonder,' mused HG as she whispered into my ear?

'I mean it; I'm glad he's dead,' replied Lemuel as he pursued his heart's desire into the butler's pantry.

A Posh Murder: Chapter Three

SECRETS

On the direct instructions of HG, I slipped from an environment of comfort and entitlement to an underworld of toil. The dowager expected that the staff might reveal tantalising gossip relating to the tragic events of the previous day.

Previous experience of observing the contrast between the upstairs rooms of the great English country houses and those of the servants' environment prepared me well for the scene as I entered the kitchen.

The master of the house being in residence meant that the inside staff had to have finished their own meal by 6.30 pm, to ready themselves to finish preparations and serve dinner at 8.00 pm on the dot.

On this occasion, however, the kitchen staff looked markedly relaxed, and a sense of genial bonhomie prevailed. I soon realised the solution to this puzzle lay in neither the butler nor the housekeeper being present. Instead, the servants' table rested in the jovial arms of Doris Lovejoy.

Doris possessed that rare combination of authority and kindness. Cross her in professional matters related to her kitchen or cooking and she would bring down the house upon the transgressor. Work hard and admit any mistakes and the cook might treat one as a wayward child requiring instruction.

Doris left me with one lasting impression that was unlike the typical characterisation of female cooks found in penny dreadful magazines, popular in some social circles. There they are often short and rotund, with a liking for sherry.

No, Doris Lovejoy was a tall, slim, elegant woman with delicate long fingers and penetrating blue eyes. A woman who, I would hazard a guess, was early into her fifth decade. Presenting herself in a brilliant white starched apron and hat, Doris ruled her domain without equal.

As I took my allotted seat near the head of the table, commensurate with being a visitor, I glimpsed Mable Popkiss, assistant cook, back at Drakeford Old Hall. HG had sent her ahead to assist Doris with the colonel's guests.

Invited to say Grace, I willingly obliged, keeping it short as I noticed several staff members looking at the shepherd's pie with ravenous eyes. Within a minute, plates filled, the gossip began.

Meanwhile, I satisfied myself by making conversation with the cook by asking what delights she'd prepared for the colonel and his guests.

'Oxtail soup, then Beef Wellington followed by Eton Mess, which is the master's favourite,' Doris replied as she monitored the shepherd's pie to ensure each of the staff received their fair share.

'It appears a happy household,' I ventured. 'That is, apart from dreadful recent events.'

My combined question and statement elicited not more than a sympathetic nod from the cook as she gave one footman a stern look for taking a third slice of freshly baked crusty bread.

Events then took their own course when one of the younger parlour maids exclaimed, 'I know, let's all play *Guess the Murderer!*'

I looked to Doris, expecting her to reprimand the girl.

Not so; instead, she merely cautioned all present to be on their guard for the return of the butler or housekeeper. 'You know what they're like.'

A ripple of conspiratorial giggles swept the long pine table as the staff looked one way, then the other, to check the coast was clear.

'Who's going first?' said the parlour maid.

'You are, Peggy. It's your idea.'

I watched the eager staff applaud as the young girl got to her feet, only for Doris to reprimand them for making too much noise, which might, she warned, bring unwanted attention to their proceedings.

'I think that Lemuel Norris person did it, you know; biffed Mr Bagley and killed him and all that.'

Several staff members appeared to agree, given the vigorousness with which they nodded. 'I heard him say he'd kill himself if Miss Dosett wouldn't have him. My bet is he got rid of his rival.'

'What about Mr Blowers? I heard the butler tell the butcher what he'd overheard the man say about that Ambrose chap,' said another.

Then a young maid, who I took to be not yet fifteen, slowly stood, her cheeks flushed with nervousness. 'Well, that's nothing. I saw Mr Peregrine watching Miss Dosett on the landing. He didn't see me but was having a right old look. Scary if you ask me.'

I should explain that the maid identified Peregrine Percival-Travers, the colonel's son. Where no title exists, staff often refer to members of their employer's family by prefixing a first name with the relevant pronoun as a mark of respect.

The maid's revelation caused much murmuring among the staff as one debated with another about the relative guilt of each party mentioned.

'Well, that's nothing,' said the boot boy. 'I was having a fag with Stan this morning and he said he hated them all and good riddance.'

The room erupted into laughter as the boy, who I estimated to be no older than fourteen years, caught the cook's eye, who summoned him to her side. 'You are much too young to smoke, my lad, let alone gossip. Now, tell me, what else did Stan Price say?'

The staff clearly appreciated the cook's indulgence of the scrawny boy, whose hair appeared not to have seen a comb this side of Easter.

Unfortunately, before I gathered further intelligence, the room fell into an immediate stony silence, which I took to mean either the butler or housekeeper, or both, had returned.

The sound of a gruff voice behind me confirmed matters. 'To your duties immediately or we shall be late serving dinner. May I remind you that this house is never late serving dinner. Get to it.'

While I huddled with the dowager as other houseguests mingled for pre-dinner drinks, the drawing room took on a different guise as ladies' formal dresses shimmered in the light and men's formal attire lent an air of gilded authority.

HG listened carefully as I relayed the information gleaned from the servants' tea, in particular, mention of the gardener and the peculiar behaviour of Peregrine.

'We must track both down as a matter of urgency to see what they have to say for themselves,' she said, all the while watching the other guests.

On one occasion, I asked the dowager about her habit of people watching. From this enquiry, I learned a valuable lesson in reading a person's body language, particularly when the individual is under stress. HG maintained that facial twitches, a hand momentarily covering the mouth while speaking or, among other signs, a person averting their eyes under interrogation, might point to guilt.

As I began my own observations, HG drew my attention to Fredrick Blowers, who appeared to be glaring at Lemuel Norris, who never took his eyes off Rowena Dosett.

'Notice that Fredrick does not look at the young lady, only Lemuel. What does this tell you?'

Aware of being tested by my tutor, I redoubled my observations to pick up subtle clues that might give away the man's intention.

After several seconds and a further prompt form the dowager, I observed that the former acted as an animal at the top of the food chain thinking about their next meal, whereas the latter, Lemuel, looked pitiful as he watched Rowena giggle in conversation with Watkins-Simms the elder as though having not a care in the world.

HG rebuked me for missing one vital clue. While

accepting my assessment of Frederick Blowers, she required that I re-evaluate my deductions concerning Lemuel. 'Do you not see the hatred in his eyes, his stiff posture, as if a coiled spring?'

On closer inspection, I withdrew my earlier comments on the fellow and apologised to HG for missing several vital components of the man's demeanour.

'Worry not,' came the dowager's reply. 'Take this as a lesson in questioning what you think you're observing with what is actually taking place.'

I now observed a man rebuffed by the love of his life and scorned by his contemporaries. What might such a man be capable of? HG had long held the view that all men, and women, were capable of the greatest feats of strength, brutality, and deceit under certain circumstances.

Could it be that beneath Lemuel's timid appearance hid a monster capable of murder? After all, perhaps killing becomes easier and if so, might Lemuel now have his sights on Watkins-Simms, the elder, who at this very moment beguiled the innocence of the young lady?

As I conveyed my new outlook on the situation, HG congratulated me for a willingness to admit my failings and learn from them. A lesson I learned repeatedly over the many years our association continued.

HG's attention once again wandered as Whipple surreptitiously entered the drawing room. 'Oh dear,' sighed the dowager.

Whipple, now shorn of his day suit, collar and tie, appeared in a dinner suit at least two sizes too big for the man. 'I swear the butler did it on purpose to humiliate me,' spat the inspector as he hid his baggy frame behind HG in the large bay window recess of the fine room.

'Not at all, Arthur. You look a picture of elegance, does he not, Rex?'

How was I to respond? Perhaps lie and give the fellow some temporary comfort, or be truthful, reinforcing all that Whipple already believed the case to be? 'You represent all that's fine about an English gentleman, Chief Inspector,' I replied, before averting my eyes for fear of giving the game away.

Thankfully, further embarrassment was stayed by the butler banging the dinner gong precisely on the stroke of eight.

'I take it you don't require a second hot meal in the space of ninety minutes, so I suggest you catch up with Mable to see if she has gleaned anything from her colleagues besides what you deduced in the servants' hall.'

With that, the dowager hitched up her skirts a little to make perambulation easier and avoid a tangle with her white satin slipper shoes. Whipple thrust both hands into his pockets to keep the oversized trousers loaned by the colonel from descending to the ground and hid behind HG's skirts.

Back in the kitchen, things were quiet as the cook put the finishing touches to the Eton Mess and placed it in the dining room servery via a dumbwaiter in the far corner of the sizeable kitchen.

'Have you seen Mable?' I asked.

Doris smiled and pointed to the small courtyard. Thinking she'd spotted my affection for Mable, I hid my blushes and proceeded at pace across the stone floor and exited a small scullery that led off the kitchen via a heavy wooden door.

———

223

'What are you doing sneaking up on a girl like that? Rex Sutherland? Call yourself a gentleman?'

After being mildly amused at catching Mable unawares, I quickly realised she did not think the matter funny in the slightest.

It took some abject apologies and cajoling for me to get back into the excellent books of a woman I was most fond of, though I have to say I suspected Mable of laying it on thick to maximise my embarrassment.

'Shush,' I said, guarding her against using my surname in public.

Having glanced around the deserted courtyard and giving me a most curious look, her only response was, 'So the dowager hasn't told them who you really are, then?'

The matter was not something I wished discussed, so I changed the subject, which Mable seemed not to object to, save for a shake of her head and a certain tutting noise made too loudly for my comfort.

'Aside from what the staff said at tea, have you any gossip for me?' My question seemed at first to shock Mable, before a rakish smile spread across her wonderful features.

'Funny you should ask that, but you know why the butler and housekeeper were absent from the servants' hall, don't you?'

I have to say one of my pet hates revolves around a person answering a question with a different question. Tempted to say that if I knew I wouldn't be asking, I tempered the urge to save annoying the wonderful Mable for the second time in as many minutes.

'No, I don't,' I replied, giving Mable the perfect opportunity to share her secret.

'They are having an affair. Yes, it's true. Doris Lovejoy said so.'

Knowing the cook's word to be unimpeachable, I pressed my enquiry. It seemed the two had known each other for some time, though the housekeeper had only recently joined the family after many years' service in a big house somewhere in Northumberland.

'And cook says she didn't get a reference, so the butler fixed it so he did the interview.'

My astonishment that a butler might conduct such an interview instead of the lady of the house clearly showed by my reaction.

'Cook says Augustine Percival-Travers is three sheets to the wind and leaves such matters to the man so she can concentrate on… well, no one seems to know what she concentrates on.'

'Anything else?' I responded, hoping to escape further detail of the curmudgeonly butler and surly housekeeper's nocturnal meanderings.

'Well,' replied Mable. 'That Peregrine chap watches people. He never talks to them, just watches, like.'

I thought a pattern emerging concerning several of the houseguests and family members. However, I could make neither head nor tail of what these trends pointed to.

For the remaining few minutes of peace I had with Mable, we talked about what we might like to do in the future and lamented the burden we each bore concerning our first or surname.

'I shall be glad to marry. Who wants a surname like Popkiss? I hate it and want rid of the thing.'

I enquired if the possession of a decent last name was all a likely candidate need offer. Mable took several seconds before adding that the man must be kind, worldly-wise and not mind too much about her passion for crocheting.

Before I had the chance to offer my own credentials, a breathless groundsman burst into the courtyard.

'Thank the Lord someone's here. There is a body of a man in the lake.'

Grab your copy...

vinci-books.com/poshmurder